ANGÉLIQUE VILLENEUVE

TRANSLATED FROM THE FRENCH
BY ADRIANA HUNTER

Peirene

Les Fleurs
d'hiver

AUTHOR

Born in Paris in 1965, Angélique Villeneuve lived in Sweden and India before returning to her native France. The author of eight novels, she has also written numerous children's books. *Les Fleurs d'hiver*, which was published by Éditions Phébus in 2014, won four literary prizes: the 2014 Prix Millepages, the 2015 Prix La Passerelle and Prix de la Ville de Rambouillet and the 2016 Prix du Livre de Caractère de Quintin. Villeneuve's novel *Maria*, published by Éditions Grasset in 2018, won the Grand Prix SGDL for fiction. Her most recent work, *La Belle Lumière*, a fictional account of the life of Helen Keller's mother, was published by Éditions Le Passage in 2020. *Winter Flowers* is the first of her books to be translated into English.

TRANSLATOR

An award-winning British translator, Adriana Hunter has translated over ninety books from French, mostly works of literary fiction. She won the 2011 Scott Moncrieff Prize for her translation of *Beside the Sea* by Véronique Olmi (Peirene Press, 2010) and the 2013 French-American Foundation and Florence Gould Foundation Translation Prize for her translation of Hervé Le Tellier's *Eléctrico W*, and her translations have been shortlisted twice for the Independent Foreign Fiction Prize (now the International Booker Prize). Hunter has translated three other books for Peirene Press: *Under the Tripoli Sky* by Kamal Ben Hameda (2014), *Reader for Hire* by Raymond Jean (2015) and *Her Father's Daughter* by Marie Sizun (2016).

Peirene

ANGÉLIQUE VILLENEUVE

TRANSLATED FROM THE FRENCH
BY ADRIANA HUNTER

Winter Flowers

First published in Great Britain in 2021 by
Peirene Press Ltd
17 Cheverton Road
London N19 3BB
www.peirenepress.com

First published under the original French title *Les Fleurs d'hiver* in 2014 by Éditions Phébus, Paris, France.

Copyright © Libella, Paris, 2014

This translation © Adriana Hunter 2021

Angélique Villeneuve asserts her moral right to be identified as the author of this work in accordance with the Copyright, Designs and Patents Act 1988.

ISBN 978-1-908670-67-0

This book is a work of fiction. Names, characters, businesses, organizations, places and events are either the product of the author's imagination or used fictitiously. Any resemblance to actual persons, living or dead, events or locales is entirely coincidental.

Designed by Sacha Davison Lunt
Cover illustration by Caroline McArthur
Typeset by Tetragon, London
Printed and bound by T J Books, Padstow, Cornwall

The content of this book represents the views of the author only and is her sole responsibility. The European Commission and the Agency do not accept any responsibility for use that may be made of the information it contains.

Co-funded by the
Creative Europe Programme
of the European Union

Supported using public funding by
ARTS COUNCIL
ENGLAND

To Michel Villeneuve

1

She hears nothing. Senses nothing. It just happens out of nowhere.

The child is on the bed playing dead, and Jeanne, kneeling beside her, soaks the edge of the cloth in the remains of some water and reaches for an arm.

Léonie tries to avoid being washed, as she always does. Lying inert, as heavy as her young body will allow, she blinks, wrinkles her nose and, slightly raising her upper lip to reveal two gap teeth, darts out the shiny tip of her white-spotted tongue.

Jeanne straightens and studies the child in the half-darkness of the room.

Léonie.

Léo.

What's left to her.

Jeanne's hands are dulled with work, her back is stiff. And as she closes her eyes, and relaxes her head and shoulders, all her in-held breath comes out at once in a hoarse cry that would leave anyone who heard it struggling to say whether it expressed pleasure or pain.

Through the thick fabric of her skirt, something thin rolls from right to left on the floor under her kneecap, most likely a twisted vine tendril that the child played with idly when she came home from nursery school a little earlier.

She'll have to light the lamp.

Léo. Her thin fingers are stiff and grey from the sort of cold that steals over a body when it stays motionless. Jeanne leans forward and breathes a hot sigh onto the palms of their four hands held together. She keeps her eyes on the screwed-up little face, waiting for the beginnings of a smile. First with the ends of stray hairs that have escaped from her plaited bun and then with her eyelashes, she skims the child's writhing chest, the areas of skin that her knitted top lays bare.

Aquiver with laughter, the child's body is suddenly slapped by a sound coming through the wall: the door to their neighbour's lodging being slammed shut. Sidonie lumbering home and making sure everyone knows.

Léo shudders, she probably really has caught cold now. It would be too stupid if she fell ill. The flu's been attacking left, right and centre for the last few weeks. A woman Jeanne knew at the workshop died in the space of three days in late September. Spanish flu. Everyone's talking about it and people tremble just at the mention of its exotic name.

Everyone knows you should never be in pain or cold or frightened on purpose.

So Jeanne huddles up against Léo, her trunk flattening heavily, stopping the child moving. She breathes her warmth into Léo's ear, the crook of her neck. She slides her cheek

8

along her ribs, sniffing with her mouth as if it were a nose and catching Léonie's smell, a smell like no one else's, not even her father's now-lost smell.

The sounds of the outside world melt away around the edges of the bed, swallowed by the warm rush of their combined bloodstreams.

It's already very cold on this late October evening and, pulling herself together, Jeanne quickly finishes washing Léo. First her face, behind her ears, next her hands, held open and then turned over one after the other, all rubbed with the damp cloth where the traces of previous washing sessions can still be read in the yellow light cast by the lamp she's just lit. The dark tide of their shared filth is overlaid here and there by long trails that look like bloodstains.

This is because, ever since the busy season started up again, a fine dust has coated her flower-maker's fingers and hangs over every part of the room, a veil of the notorious 'bad red' used for petals. It is this red that shades the cloth, while the earthy green of the paper she uses stains her mouth, forcing Jeanne to spit out foul saliva at regular intervals. When she's winding green paper strips around the vine tendrils that act as stalks, she uses her own mouth hundreds of times a day to moisten the pliable ends which are saturated with lead sulphate.

Léo is dressed again, her thin little legs thickened by several pairs of long socks worn one on top of the other. Squatting before the stove, Jeanne delves inside it for anything that might rekindle a vague whisper of orange, just enough to reheat yesterday's stew to an acceptable temperature.

She mustn't stir up the coal too much, mustn't waste a thing. The posters outside keep saying so. Everything must be made to last.

And she definitely hopes this new winter won't be as harsh as the last, when she sometimes had to work wearing all the clothes she owned in order to keep in the heat. One evening she even put the eiderdown over the top, improvising a sort of warm tent that threatened to slide off at any moment. Sitting there at the table, which she'd moved so that her chair could be hard up against the stove, she looked like a huge creature made of dirty washing, with two black paws of coiled wool poking out.

With half a gross of these red dahlias to finish before morning, her day's far from over. Like so many women who work from home, Jeanne struggles to put in her ten or eleven hours a day without staying up at least part of the night. On top of her work, there's the child who needs taking to school, the shopping, deliveries, housework and the stove.

While Jeanne ekes out the stock with water, Léo hums between her teeth, hardly making a sound, her nose pressed up to her rag doll's face. She's placid and almost always cheerful. She plays with her things alone, in her little corner of tiled floor. And because she's still not asking for her supper, Jeanne decides to get back to work straight away.

She opens the door to the landing, just a crack. Then she won't have to get up when Sidonie comes a little later to collect the boxes that she'll drop off at the workshop on her way to deliver her calico aprons.

The seamstress will simply let herself in without knocking, as she usually does. The two of them will sit together for a while, drinking a small glass of milk each. Sharing the dregs of a bottle of wine, if Sidonie has any left.

The room is filled with flickering lamplight that seems to mirror Léo's never-ending sing-song, and the smell of boiled and reboiled stew slowly rises, catching at Jeanne's nostrils and numbing her fingers.

Perhaps that's why she hasn't picked up on anything.

2

For a start, she doesn't hear the footsteps, even though the staircase in her building is very vocal; its treads creak terribly. Nothing seems to break through the rampart of Jeanne's concentration when she's immersed in her flowers.

Neither does she suspect the silent, unseen trickles of sweat on this man standing, waiting. She's unaware of his altered posture, the painful tensing of his shoulders and neck, his wrists.

And yet he's been there for at least ten minutes, utterly still. After the warped wooden stairs, it's now his whole body, his nocturnal presence, that creaks as he grimaces in a silence streaked with blue light.

His clothes – the stiff military coat that he's buttoned all the way up, the serge trousers and black hobnailed boots – are things he hasn't worn or even seen for months, no, come to think of it, years. All the same, they're still his, he recognizes them.

But he fills them so badly. The frame that they envelop has, imperceptibly, changed. When he came to put them on, he hesitated; perhaps he should have chosen civilian clothes, but he has nothing left from... from before – he alone has survived from his past life. And beyond his outward appearance he's not sure what sort of state he's survived in, when all's said and done.

Sitting at her table, Jeanne senses nothing. It has to be said that the huge red dahlias, whose wound-like qualities are accentuated by the light from the oil lamp, completely absorb her in a swirl of scarlet. The repeated gestures gradually steal over her whole body, leaving no part of her in which she can drift. When Jeanne sleeps or closes her eyes, when she's absent in mind or body, she knows this much: the flowers are still there and always will be.

There are now only a few dozen left of the last gross of dahlias she has to make. Two dozen. Perhaps three dozen of the six that she needs to finish before the end of the day. She's nearing her goal. Sidonie will be able to come over, conversation will flow, she'll let go. The day will be complete.

After a meal of stock with three slices of carrot and a memory of stringy meat floating in it, Léo has finally fallen asleep with her head laid delicately next to her pillow and one arm thrust out. Jeanne needn't keep an eye on her now.

Meanwhile, on the other side of the barely open door, all he can see is a narrow strip to the right of the doorway, where the room opens onto the pitch-dark storage area.

At first he thought it a little odd, this unshut door. Was Jeanne even inside? He was worried. He'd heard so many stories about women left behind.

But, straining his ears, he soon clearly hears the familiar clicking sounds. Since he left, he's grown used to listening more attentively. For possible threats, or reassurances. Now, to his enormous relief, Jeanne's soft music is restored to him, unchanged and true. The rustle of her fingers as she picks through boxes for little groupings of petals, sepals or leaves that she's already dyed. Her very distinctive humming, like the buzz of a wasp. The selection of shaping balls that she heats and wields deftly. The pliers that she puts down and picks up again.

It all comes back to him.

What's different is his fear. But still.

Still.

Fear.

Neither here on rue de la Lune nor before in Belleville had he ever been frightened. Not of her, not like this.

All at once he remembers the cheese. Here in his canvas bag, a big hunk of it, hard and a hearty orange colour; he's been keeping it for days. This cheese, he thinks to himself, this cheese could be his entry ticket, a gift from one of the magi. The swell of his knapsack in his hand encourages him to make a move.

He puts his hand flat on the wood and pushes, gently at first and then, taking a deep breath, with hearty conviction.

That's that.

He's pushed the door open but is still on the landing, standing very upright in the darkness. And Jeanne looks up quickly, her eyes still drenched in the red of the dahlias.

*

If anyone asked them now, asked him or her, they probably wouldn't know. Wouldn't know what exactly happened. What they thought and felt in that moment.

Perhaps, yes, she would have said that Toussaint's taller. Because without thinking, idiotically, it strikes her that he's grown during the war, that, after years of absence, this man who's being returned to her takes up the full height and breadth of the doorway.

In the past thirty months, the only people she's seen appear in that space – Sidonie, Léo, Mother Birot and the caretaker – are made of different stuff, no doubt about it. And right now Toussaint's puffing himself up as much as he can, expanding his lungs, sucking in his stomach and tensing his long thigh muscles, taut, as if anticipating a blow.

At first Jeanne stays rooted to her chair, entirely consumed with watching him and avoiding him. She knows what she should see, though, where she should look, but it bounces about, slips away from her. What she does grasp is that he's taller, and handsome in his uniform, and unfamiliar too.

She doesn't think, He's here, she thinks, It's here. This unknown thing that's coming home to her. That she's dreaded, and longed for. It's here. It's going to come in, it's going to make its life with her, and with Léo too, it will come here, into this room that the two of them have shared so little since they left Belleville.

He was far away, he was no longer made of flesh and words. But now it's here and he, Toussaint, is much taller than before.

Jeanne stammers without making a sound, gathers herself, wipes her green mouth, makes up her mind to put down her pliers and stand up, given that he isn't coming in and is waiting, standing so rigid. She doesn't cry out, she can't, isn't even startled, but all the same, Léo's now sitting up in bed and staring at them, first one then the other, puffy-faced, dishevelled and apprehensive.

Toussaint has chosen his moment.

He hoped for help from the shadows, and here they are around him, in all their feathery softness. It's as if the October night behind him is supporting him. The room in front of him is soft, saturated with everyday smells.

He's been ready for so long that he could have arrived earlier. But he was aiming for after dark, lingering, delaying the moment when rue de la Lune would open up before him. He came on foot – not that he's used to walking any distance now, or to exertion of any kind; not that he's the same as before. It took him a long time. He didn't count the hours. On the streets, and the wide Grands Boulevards in particular, the traffic was not as heavy as it used to be, but there were still people about.

They must have peered at him; some passer-by or other, whether civilian or military, most likely went so far as to call out to him. But he heard nothing, saw nothing. He hunkered down inside himself. People walking past were reduced to a single mass, alive and seething.

He was aware of the cold, the damp smell, the shifting draughts and colours produced by the movements of trams and motor taxis. The sounds of Paris. Before going out he'd felt he would never get used to them again; well, he would, but only slowly. And now here it all was, just like before, or almost, so not that daunting after all. It was only people he no longer saw.

He just kept walking, sometimes losing his way, switching to the other side of the road or to another street for no reason, but making his way. And in the end, caught up in his own momentum, he stepped into this humble building in a neighbourhood he hardly knew, where his wife and daughter had been living alone for nearly three and a half years.

He was lucky. When he walked past the caretaker's well-lit lodge without giving his name, she didn't notice a thing and so didn't call out to stop him.

Léo has finally slipped timidly out of bed. Jeanne glances at her and risks taking a few steps. It's her turn.

It isn't far to go. Her home – well, their home – isn't very big. One room flanked by a storage area where she keeps her belongings.

That's all. But it's a long way. It's too far and too near.

Jeanne walks towards him and her eyes jitter. She'd like them to be steadfast, but they leap about, wilfully.

And that flash of white up ahead burns them.

She'd like to smile and open her arms, but feels doltish, hot, redder than the big red dahlia abandoned back there on the table. She wishes she were all kindness, filled to the brim with him. She'd like to be able to touch Toussaint, to tilt an open face towards his, she'd like to feel one single emotion and to simulate nothing, but now everything's a muddle, nothing's as she planned it, not that she had planned anything, hadn't wanted to think about it, couldn't believe that it really would happen one day.

Because she can't whoop, can't stand squarely in front of her husband, reach up on tiptoe and kiss him, she goes right up to him, puts her arms around him, rests her cheek against the serge of his coat and waits.

3

She remembers mobilization day. Afterwards, Jeanne and her neighbours and masses of other people, including some with whom she would never have exchanged a single word in normal times, endlessly chewed over it.

Of course they all remembered what they were doing that Saturday in August 1914, and where they were when they first saw the posters, heard the tocsin or were told by someone better informed than themselves.

Sidonie was told by her son Eugène, who'd heard the news from his boss, the butcher on rue Thorel.

Jeanne and Sidonie live across the landing from each other. At the top of the stairs on the fourth floor, Sidonie occupies two gloomy rooms where she has toiled at her work since the time of her marriage to Albert, sixteen years earlier. She is the older of the two women.

When, in the spring of 1915, Jeanne was turned out of her rented room in Belleville and came to live here with her daughter, it was Sidonie who explained everything to her, showing her where and how to fetch water, how best to use the latrines on the half landing, and what to think of the tenants on the first floor and of the shifty coral dealer who still rented the small ground-floor shop at the time; Sidonie who ensured that Jeanne was in favour with the butcher, where her son worked as an apprentice. She too who tried, but without success in this instance, to lure her over to the church.

So the two women see a good deal of each other. They share what little they have, the coffee and heating, the lack of coffee and lack of heating. The silences and absences. Their meagre meals too, occasionally. Together they've discussed the best way to peel vegetables, to waste as little as possible. They've learned to cook the fat and the bones, to make briquettes for their stoves out of old newspaper. Last year they grew a cabbage in a broken cooking pot on Jeanne's balcony and ate it, just the two of them, one leaf at a time.

With the war, orders for women who work from home have become increasingly sparse and unreliable. Jeanne is lucky: she's qualified, valued and has managed to keep working nearly year-round. Granted, her arms are not as heavy-laden, her pockets not as well filled, but the two women are tackling this together. Because the department store that outsources some of its sewing to Sidonie isn't far from the flower-making workshop, and because the women can't afford to pay a delivery boy, they help each other out with deliveries.

Eugène was seventeen on mobilization day – in other words, he was spared. But as soon as the news was announced he told his mother that he didn't want to wait to be called up.

He was going to enlist. And one evening in early September the lad vanished.

A card arrived.

Eugène was in the Ardennes.

At that stage of the war people were still optimistic. It would all be over in a few weeks, everyone kept saying.

That was what people said, it would all be done and dusted. We'll crush them. Joffre had announced that there wouldn't even be time to make helmets for soldiers: he'd be wiping the floor with the Boche within two months anyway. There wasn't really anything to worry about. The boy would be home soon, and he'd go back to working for the butcher on rue Thorel like a good boy.

But Sidonie wept. What had she ever done to the good Lord? And some people in the neighbourhood couldn't help but ask themselves the selfsame question. She or perhaps someone close to her really must have done something to upset the good Lord. Such an ordeal couldn't simply be down to fate, and so many punishments piled one on top of the other must surely have been dealt out to appease the wrath of a grievously offended creator.

What precisely the sin was, nobody knew. But that was beside the point. Come September 1914, no one on rue de la Lune or beyond had the heart to jeer at Sidonie's anguish and wailing. She was to be pitied, the poor woman. Every household was missing one or two men, or even more, but when the seamstress started sobbing in the street people nodded and discreetly held their tongues.

*

Sidonie spent much of mobilization day in the nearby church. In the months to come, Jeanne often wondered why the church had been given that name: Our Lady of Good News.

For Mother Birot, Jeanne's neighbour on the left, it was a different story.

She had never married and never had children, and the only man she'd ever wept for in her whole life was her father, whom she'd described in a few brief, definitive words to her companions in freezing hardship, one night in February 1917, when the rigours of the weather had forced the three women and the child to share the same bed.

For years now Mother Birot had made a living sorting dirty washing for a large laundry on boulevard Poissonnière. Despite her age and her sickly complexion, in February 1915 she – along with more than a thousand other women – was taken on by a camouflage workshop in the 20th arrondissement.

Here, surrounded by girls a third or a quarter her age, she worked eleven hours a day, six days a week. And when she arrived home on rue de la Lune in the evening, Mother Birot was bone-weary but sated by the soothing notion of having served something greater than herself.

Mobilization day.

Jeanne casts her mind back to it. A sunny day that had been too luminously bright, its contours blurred. If she talks about it so much, with anyone and everyone, then it is to find out once and for all what happened. As if other people's stories could somehow, implicitly, tell her own.

What did she make of it, Jeanne, when she set off to take a delivery to the workshop and noticed a gathering outside the brasserie? A poster had been stuck to the wall. She took her turn, edging closer, and, by elbowing her way through, managed to read it.

The thought that Toussaint would go off to war did not occur to her straight away. In any event, there was absolutely no mention of war on the poster. Right in the middle of it, in large letters, were the words 'All men'. That she does remember. All men.

The crowd around her teemed with opinions and nodding heads, and, in her fearful, overwrought state, seemed to constitute a single body from which she had been excluded all along.

All men. That included neither Jeanne nor her child, for sure. As for Toussaint, of course Toussaint was a man, that wasn't the question.

But it wasn't the same, it didn't count. He was hers.

The muddled notion that the term 'All men' had no bearing whatsoever on him may have been fanciful, but then the idea that they would all set out at once, all these men, in a single great long herd, was equally absurd. Toussaint was a husband and father. Léonie wasn't yet seven months old. Toussaint belonged to them.

Jeanne had shaken her head. The poster was about another world. Other people.

Then, her eyes flitting haphazardly, unable to make up her mind to read the text in the correct order, from left to right and top to bottom, she had caught other words: 'On pain of punishment under the full weight of the law'.

What on earth were they thinking, for goodness' sake? Neither she nor Toussaint seemed guilty to her.

At this point someone shoved into her, into Jeanne and her load of brand-new boxed clematis. The notched edge of a straw boater jarred against her temple and she was carried along by the crowd, far away from the poster with its flags, far away from All men.

Trudging slowly, she made her delivery. No one there was talking about mobilization. Or perhaps she didn't want to hear. She dropped off the flowers, had her pay-book signed and took the materials she needed for her next order.

Back at home, she picked up the baby, whom she'd left with a neighbour, and put her straight to bed. And instead of sitting down to work, she started rifling feverishly through the sideboard. It was here, she remembered, that the military record book was kept. She opened it as if it was sure to give her an answer, or at least confirmation of her intuition.

She read:

Caillet, Toussaint.
Class of 1907.
HAIR: dark blond.
EYES: blue.

FOREHEAD: vertical gradient, average height, average
   width.
NOSE: straight, positioned high above the mouth, aver-
   age height, average protuberance, average width.
FACE: oval.
HEIGHT: 1.79 metres.

Under 'Additional physiognomic information', someone
had put:

MOUTH: full.
CHIN: prominent.

Further on, it said that Toussaint could read and write. It
said he couldn't swim.

And every page was littered with the word she refused to
acknowledge, leaping out at her. Table of the man's measure-
ments, the man's year group, the man's personal belongings.

Standing by the light of the window, flicking too quickly
through the pages, Jeanne had trouble breathing. She didn't
recognize Toussaint. Even in the photograph he had an
enigmatic half-smile, as if he could be hiding something
from her.

If this record book, which contained within it a mobilization booklet, was irrefutable proof that Toussaint was
included in All men, then it needed to be kept hidden until
this was over, this whim, and the poster forgotten.

She considered it for a good hour, with the book stowed
next to the warmth of her body, between her skin and her

blouse. And then she didn't dare. In the irrational hope that Toussaint wouldn't find it there, she put it back in the bottom of the sideboard, her skin still cloyed with anxious sweat.

She didn't work well that afternoon, fidgeting on her chair as she made up an order of anemones, unintentionally catching snatches of hubbub from the street through the wide-open window. She wished something would happen there, outside, that something would erupt. Bring the world back to its senses.

She needed to buckle down to her flowers, get on with them. When she pulled herself together and finally settled to her work, she was in such a hurry to crimp the petals that she overheated the metal balls and several of the white petals – now misshapen and rust-marked by the iron – were wasted.

She tutted impatiently, trying to revert to her steady, familiar movements. She needed to get back to where she should be, get her hands under control again. When you have work in August, it's better not to count your sorrows: the summer was the dead season for flower-makers, before the rush for winter flowers in October.

Since leaving her apprenticeship, where she'd qualified as a maker of 'naturals', Jeanne had worked from home, for a reputable firm. She was better off than many others, but in a bad year she could be laid off for several consecutive weeks in the summer. From June to September at the very least you had to be sure never to drag your heels. If you gave up, if the desert opened up, you could always join the girls doing feather work. But flowers, especially the naturals, would always pay a little better than feathers.

Apparently some girls at the workshop had been reduced to making celluloid flowers. Funeral wreaths are in fashion all year round. But even before the war Jeanne hadn't wanted to do that.

And so she sat at her table and battled on.

Mobilization.

She was still thinking about it.

The war.

What exactly was a war? An enormous grey mass, intangible and impossible. Incomprehensible. Those words – the ones on the poster and in other people's mouths – weren't for them.

And yet, despite her mulishness and the energy she put into juggling a thousand irrefutable arguments in her head to prove that this was just a passing fancy, an overhasty reaction from the government or some obscure military affair, her conviction that she and Toussaint would be spared fractured as the hours went by.

At the end of the day, after suckling Léo, she carried the well-fed child on her hip and went to stand outside the shoe factory on rue Pixérécourt, where Toussaint then worked on the assembly line. She didn't come all the way over here very often; she normally had too much to do with her own work. But of course, and Jeanne was as aware of this as anyone else, 1 August 1914 wasn't a normal day.

Just before reaching the factory, she stopped off at the nearby Bellevilloise cooperative to buy watercress, which Toussaint loved, horsemeat salami and macaroni. As she came out, as if by some malicious twist of fate, the street sign for the tiny no through road where the cooperative stood jumped out at her. Future Street (dead end), it said, and Jeanne looked away.

She was not the only one waiting by the factory door. There they were, the wives, mostly in groups of two or three, all of them worried.

Jeanne scanned the tide of workmen that finally streamed onto the pavement, and when she spotted Toussaint in the middle, engrossed in conversation, animated, she faltered and thought to herself that, no, she'd been wrong.

When it came down to it, surrounded by the cutters and assemblers, those who stitched and finished and stuck on soles, wasn't her husband just one among All men?

Frightened by the commotion, little Léonie had let her downy head loll into the crook of Jeanne's neck.

And all at once Toussaint had turned towards them, frowning. His gaze swept indifferently over the buildings and then landed on Jeanne, who was leaning against the house opposite. It collided with her as she stood motionless with her baby, her plaited bun and her dark, helpless eyes. His gaze came to rest on her and his face filled with such a life force, such a fierce light, that Jeanne clenched her fists.

She was right, Toussaint would never be swallowed up in the ocean of All men, she would be proved right, he wouldn't go.

4

As soon as he was admitted to Val-de-Grâce military hospital, Toussaint sent his wife a brief letter.

'I want you not to come.'

Those were his words.

It was clear, definitive. It invited no reply, and Jeanne sent none.

Since then, the wounded man had sent a card regularly every month, invariably saying nothing more than that he was in good health.

When Jeanne had first read this letter, in January 1917, she was baffled, disappointed; then, as she grasped what his words really meant, stung as if by a huge wasp. No one knew how long a healing process like his might take, and nine months had already trickled by since his last leave.

On the wall, above her head, hung his portrait, Toussaint the soldier. She could no longer look at it.

Even so, she realized after a few hours that she was relieved, not only because he was alive, being treated, out of danger and in the warm, but also, perhaps, thankful that she need not be confronted with him.

With it.

Not now. She wasn't ready. Besides, she didn't know how to prepare for it, or even if there actually was any way to prepare for such a thing.

She thought she felt calmer. She opened the iron box where she'd been keeping her letters since the beginning of the war and, on top of the official letter that had informed her of his injury a month earlier, she gently stowed these words that have kept her away ever since.

The weather had been especially harsh at the start of that year. After the letter arrived, the cold and the daily struggle had completely consumed Jeanne, mind and body. Until the cold eased and the hours in the day reclaimed some light, she had to battle to find coal or wood for her stove, and something she could cook on it.

It was high season at the time, the winter months when she made flowers for summer hats and clothes. There was still work, despite the war, and she had thrown herself into it, more so than ever. A furious anger swept over her, obliterating her entirely. Her rage swallowed down the vicious powder of the 'bad red' dye and sucked on the salts in the lead paper, her grief ruined its eyesight long into the cold nights until, befuddled and aching, she could fall fully clothed onto her bed next to the tiny Léo, a corpse released at last.

She always woke with a start first thing in the morning. She should have stirred herself, gone straight back to work, but for many months Toussaint's words tore at her. They were dark words.

I want you not to come.

Over time, the unusual construction so intrigued her that she tried to read into it what hadn't been said. Why hadn't he added 'my little darling', as he so often did, why hadn't he written, 'It's better if you don't come for now'? Or 'We need to be patient', or 'The doctor would rather we waited before you visit', or, worst of all, 'I don't want you to come'?

Toussaint hadn't chosen any of these. Perhaps he'd had enough of not wanting, because no one ever listened to him. He had told his wife what he wanted, not what he didn't want.

I want you not to come.

She tormented herself with these words. Was there a hidden meaning to his letter? Why did the 'not' smack her in the face like that, so powerfully?

And of all the words kept in the iron box, these, the most recent, were the only ones she remembered. And yet there were so many others, stacked together in the rusty-smelling shadows. The truth was they didn't say anything, those other words, they didn't convey anything. But they were there.

'My little darling'. They did say that, then.

They said, 'I'm writing'. They said, 'I'm writing to give you my news', but never really gave any.

The words had safely received the parcel with the jumper, the socks, the pâté. The words were doing well, they hoped Jeanne and the little one were too. The words fumbled for memories of life before. They said, 'The sky's very blue'.

Once or twice the words had spent three days lying in a shell hole, they'd carried sandbags all night, or kept watch through a gap in the parapet in the rain or the snow. They'd covered every inch of their skin in cresyl because of the lice that just wouldn't give up; you couldn't kill the things, the little beggars. If Jeanne could just see how much vermin there was – she wouldn't believe it, she wouldn't.

The words had received a card from their father, who'd sent ten francs. They thought that Léo must have grown a lot, changed a lot, she must be walking now and talking.

They surrendered no true facts about life at the front. And if they silenced the nightmare of his world, it wasn't only down to censorship, which proscribed any criticism, anything alarming. The words simply offered up to the reader whatever could be tolerated back home.

And they kept coming, faithfully, unfurling through the air. Thinking of her.

They waited for her letters. They said thank you. They sent kisses. And these words were usually, mostly, in the best of health.

She waited for them so impatiently. Because these words said what the two of them were, deep down. She was alive and he was alive, they were held together in their thoughts.

If the card came with dried flowers or leaves gathered by his own hand, Jeanne would pore over them motionless for many a long minute, fingering them softly, as she might have gazed at and touched his skin, his mouth.

And just as willingly, just as sincerely, she wrote back with her own lies, hiding the anguish, the loneliness, the hardship, the unstoppable flow of honeysuckle, lilac, jasmine and Noisette roses that were constantly ferried between the workshop and rue des Cascades in Belleville, where she lived at the time, or, later, rue de la Lune. She made these flowers until she was asleep on her feet, until late at night, when she felt scalding tears spill over her cheeks, because the woman who sold them always wanted more of them, and for lower and lower prices. Because she didn't have him.

She didn't mention that her hands were stiff with cold, and from the endlessly repeated movements; kept quiet about the never-ending queues for potatoes or a meagre chop that had tripled in price, the frequent trips to the welfare office at the town hall in the 20th and then the 2nd arrondissement, the miseries inflicted on her by successive caretakers, the landlord's threats, Léo's chickenpox or her cough, the coal she didn't have, the towering fever that had the two of them in its grip for days on end, first one, then the other.

And what she hid more than anything else, like a secret she wished Toussaint could read between the lines all for himself, was her stubborn longing for him.

Before the war, of course, they'd never written to each other. Paper and ink were not a means of communication. In fact they'd hardly been apart for more than a few odd days, when one of Jeanne's relatives was unwell and she needed to return to the farm in Replonges, in the Ain region, to visit her family – and then only in summer, the dead season for her work. Words written between them had never existed. And then along came the war and letters had appeared, flying from one to the other.

Their tightly packed, wavering lines inscribed in big black loops gobbled every corner of white on the card, to demonstrate that they'd said everything that could be said, that they hadn't been impersonal and had hidden nothing from each other.

These letters were dotted with spelling mistakes and mis-shapen sentences, which didn't bother Jeanne or Toussaint, because their spelling and their grammar demonstrated an ardour, a capriciousness and a tenderness that were beyond the clutches of this war, which had turned so many aspects of their lives upside down.

But the last words Jeanne had received were very different: they were claws, and she bore their scratch marks on her neck.

She pictured herself forcing her husband to say them to her out loud, looking her squarely in the eye. Would he still dare tell her that he wanted her not to come?

And then the image in her mind's eye blurred; whatever did Toussaint look like now?

When he'd come home for his second leave the previous April, in 1916, he'd already changed. He hadn't known how to convey what he'd been through 'there'. And what he saw of 'here' – the shirkers, a home life that was quiet in spite of everything, the discrepancy between his experience of the front and what the papers said about it – left him dazed. Well-wishers who hoped to share his pain with a silent pat on the shoulder triggered in him an impulse to flee, sometimes even an urge to land a punch. And when people bombarded him with questions, he couldn't answer.

I want you not to come.

She couldn't get it out of her head. But some days, miraculously, those inhibitory words eventually softened in her mind.

She spoke them quietly to herself, in the dark, said them ten and twelve and twenty times, her face buried in the eiderdown on her bed.

She said, I want you to come, and the 'not' melted away in the eiderdown's feathery folds.

She said, I want you to, and she saw things behind her closed eyelids, parts of him, movements, hollows and out-lines, the rocking action of his shoulder, his hip.

I want you to, and his slow, man's breath bloomed once more on the back of her neck, I want you, and Toussaint's body, entwined with her own, came to life again.

5

In August, old man Caillet had extricated himself from his stamping ground in Ménilmontant and gone all the way to Val-de-Grâce.

On that day – and he announces this with great pride even now – he was the first family member to see Toussaint since his last leave, twenty-eight months earlier.

Jeanne doesn't know whether her injured husband couldn't bring himself to deny his father the favour of a visit. Or whether the surgeon had finally allowed it, agreed to this visit, having previously forbidden it.

She asked no questions.

Perhaps Joseph simply turned up at the hospital door one fine morning, without warning.

Perhaps they hadn't been said, not to him. Those words.

That he was not to come.

What she does know is that old man Caillet went in the end. He went to Department 5 – Facial Injuries. He was allowed in and later came and told his daughter-in-law what little he could say about what he had seen.

Jeanne listened. She kept her secret. She didn't say that in February the year before, barely a month after her husband had been admitted to Val-de-Grâce, long before his visit, she had taken the tram and then walked to boulevard de Port-Royal. The difference was that she'd settled for pacing round in circles on the huge pavement. She kept bumping up against I want you not to come.

For a full half-hour she'd drifted up and down outside. Snow that had fallen days before still stubbornly blanketed Paris. It was fifteen degrees below freezing, it was a Sunday and everything was brittle and swirling. She thought of Léo, who was with a neighbour, waiting for her, shivering. She didn't know how to think about Toussaint.

Two shadowy creatures headed towards her along the boulevard. One pushed a barrow while the other, a stockier figure, flung shovelfuls of greyish sand onto the snow as if sowing seeds. Bundled up in old black clothes and tall black hats, their feet in wooden clogs and their hands in huge gloves, they suddenly uttered a series of strange, drawn-out yelps. Peeping from the pockets of their capes were the necks of bottles that seemed to be an integral part of their bodies. Under their hoods, Jeanne managed to make out two indistinct, steamy faces with heavy features, only vaguely identifiable as female. Because of the war, women had to stand in for men, even for tasks as harsh as this.

As the two gritters drew nearer, their movements accelerated. And when Jeanne was within their reach, the nearest of the women raised her shovel and a stream of sand and salt pelted Jeanne, savagely spattering the side of her skirt.

She flinched, repressing a scream, and fled.

*

On her way home, she glanced at a poster on a wall by the door of a wine and spirits shop. She was so shaken that the text had stayed with her for several days, clinging to her mind, covered with a thin shiny crust of ice.

The following are STRICTLY FORBIDDEN: any discouraging, undermining or critical words, or any conversations liable to weaken the patriotic effort and absolute confidence in our Leaders and our Allies.

At the time, she didn't have the strength to be angry, even less to cry. She hurried home as quickly as she could, hampered by the fact that one of the tram lines was closed.

Back at rue de la Lune, she raced up to relieve her neighbour. The old woman who'd been minding the child was surprised to see the flower-maker back so soon, but in view of Jeanne's moist eyes and tight lips she didn't dare make any comment.

When she closed the door at last and cast an eye around her room submerged in flowers, roses with their hundreds of petals and forget-me-nots, Jeanne undid her clothes and pressed a still-sleeping Léo to the warmth of her skin, inside her smock and under three layers of wool.

She rocked her.

She lulled herself along with the baby, and they reeled and swayed until nightfall.

'I want you not to come,' Toussaint had said.

When Jeanne finally put the baby to bed, biting back her tears and hissing like an angry cat, she wondered whether those very words weren't liable to weaken her patriotic effort.

He wanted her not to come.

She wouldn't come.

That year, 1917, it snowed right up until Palm Sunday.

6

Toussaint is back.

On this first evening, once her initial astonishment has passed, Jeanne settles him in the armchair that she's hastily cleared of her work things, because that's where he always automatically sat before.

The man unbuttons his coat slowly, deposits onto the tiled floor the meagre kitbag brought home from war and hospital, lays his coat over the bedhead and takes out his hunk of cheese. Meanwhile Jeanne rushes about, feeling lighter on her feet now that she's embarked on a flurry of useful-looking activity.

She leaps to the door that Toussaint didn't bother to close behind him – come on, we must run and tell Sidonie, give her the incredible news, he's here, Toussaint is, he's home. She also needs to let her know about a delivery of flowers – what do they matter now, the dahlias? Sidonie can wait. All the flowers in the world can wait. The seamstress can just stay at home this evening. Now really isn't the time to come and gossip over a cup of diluted milk or even the remains of some wine.

And anyway… and anyway, what if Toussaint was thirsty?

Everything jostles about inside Jeanne's head, her impulses, her every move. All the things that have stayed put in there, motionless and stable, are buffeted and convulsed in so many directions that she feels giddy.

With one foot already outside, she's mentally planning what she will say when she realizes that, to Sidonie, these triumphant words could play out to a very different tune, and she retreats with a ridiculous groan.

The truth is, she's filled with such terror and so many jumbled emotions that if she's not careful she'll make all sorts of blunders.

She gently closes the door. The landing and its bluish darkness disappear.

And then at last – because this is what she should have done straight away – she goes and crouches by the child, who's backed up against the bed, and she smooths her hair with the flat of her hand.

If she'd known earlier, she would have dampened the child's hair when she washed her, she'd have re-established a parting, bang in the middle. But Jeanne reaches for the child, tousled hair and all, and picks her up in her arms with a theatrical grunt.

She clears her throat, turns towards Toussaint.

Here they both are, mother and daughter, in a single body that Jeanne thinks of as proudly confident, or at least more solid when held together like this.

She says, This is your daddy.

And because the dumbstruck Léo doesn't say a word, she adds, for Toussaint's benefit, This is Léo, as if it needed pointing out, as if she could be anyone else, this child here in her arms, still warm from their bed. This is Léonie, she corrects herself, and heaves a big sigh that appears to be an achievement.

Toussaint introduces something new, not just within the walls of the small fourth-floor room, but also into Jeanne's life and, to a lesser extent, into Léo's: silence.

For the first few days, curled in a foetal position under the eiderdown or sitting in the armchair with his head lolling forward, he sleeps a great deal, although it's not clear whether he's boundlessly tired or if this withdrawal is in fact intended to eradicate his whole body.

The mother and daughter whisper around him, in the narrow spaces relinquished to them by this silence.

Jeanne isn't used to seeing her husband so economical with his movements, so passive, but she concludes that she's just no longer used to her husband, full stop. He needs a few days, maybe more.

Back in the days of the shoe factory on rue Pixérécourt, he would come home from work exhausted but with armfuls of stories spilling from him.

A new apprentice being ragged, the snarling supervisor, the workers' pay, which was being pared back in every direction week on week, Bouillet's blazing altercations with his disabled wife, Giraud's benders and banter, and Tirard's, old man Deguaque's and young Pichon's – these were all sources of endless animated conversation for Toussaint and his wife.

As he talked in the evenings, he sometimes ended up helping her by winding ribbon around stalks and preparing petals into even clusters so that she could just help herself to them.

Jeanne used to admire the precision of his sturdy fingers with their blackened nails. His tall frame felt supple and weightless in the room. He smoked the whole time. And touched her. And gave off his strong, familiar Caillet smell. He expected things. His food, his wine, his tobacco, Jeanne's roving eyes and her body there for the taking.

Since coming back he has done nothing. Right at the beginning, curious and unnerved, Jeanne asked questions, but he never replied, avoiding eye contact, nodding his head awkwardly but solemnly before turning away.

Of course, she'd suspected that the war and his injury would have changed him, but she'd never tried to imagine the scale or even the nature of this disruption. The letter he'd sent her in January 1917 had been a dark window and, once she'd stomached the pain of it, she'd made a point of not reopening it.

Like all women whose husbands or sons had been mobilized, though, she'd heard countless stories about men's homecomings. Poor women. Those who entrusted a sheep to their country were given back a lion. Someone who'd set out as a young lad was said to have come home an old man, or mad.

And there were so many, Jeanne was well aware, who would never come home at all.

*

That first evening, they have to reassemble the cot, which has been propped against the back wall since his last, long-ago leave.

The cot's metal sides have served only to dry washing behind the worktable and Léo now finds it difficult to sleep in it, peeled away from her mother. And their skins, one as soft as the other, their warmth so often mingled together in the past, call out to each other unobtrusively in an imperceptible hum that persists all through the night. They miss each other.

In the shared double bed, despite the size of the body now heavily occupying so much space, Jeanne feels colder, she feels lonelier than before the soldier's return.

They must share out their meagre provisions.

First, they must eat the orange cheese, which, Jeanne can tell from its colour, is from Holland. It would be sensible to make it last, given how unusual it is these days to have anything good to eat and, more prosaically, that fills you up.

But they finish it briskly, in an unvoiced haste, to eradicate a past full of battles and hospitals, haunted by indescribable pain. To be shot of it even sooner, Jeanne offers a good chunk of it to Sidonie and Mother Birot, who pop round one after the other to wish the convalescent well. Feeling piqued – particularly Sidonie, who, to her considerable surprise, can't get a single word out of the man or persuade him to lift the mask from his face – the two women leave, never to return.

Now she must get back to work.

This couldn't be easier for Jeanne, who finds resuming the familiar actions a relief. After ten minutes of making grooves in petals or shaping them into buds, she forgets that Toussaint is there, sleeping on and on beside her, snoring with a new amplitude and intonation, at eleven o'clock in the morning, three in the afternoon, seven in the evening.

And if the man ever keeps his eyes open, then he's busy watching them from afar, her or Léo.

Jeanne can feel a wave unfurling over her shoulders, her hands and her back, probing her bun, her neck, the folds of her dress: he's watching her. Sometimes it's the child's turn. This daughter he hasn't seen grow up, he watches her too, with miraculous, disturbing patience.

Through these late October days, whenever Jeanne or Léo looks round, Toussaint is always there, watching or sleeping.

In an attempt to curb her irritation, Jeanne takes to saturating the silence with everyday chatter and tasks. Diluting Toussaint in the pigment that bathes her flowers, she does her best to go through the motions of a reassuring day-to-day life that no longer exists.

Léo, meanwhile, is adapting.

If her father's asleep when she comes home from school, she goes straight over to him, irresistibly drawn by his magnetic face. Jeanne intercepts her, unhooks the photo from the wall and, with a finger to her lips, leads her carefully over to the inanimate body sprawled on the bed.

Léo knows the portrait well. For months now, she's hauled a chair over to study it more closely, standing squarely facing it, her chin tilted up and her hands leaning on the wallpapered walls, utterly silent.

The man she now inspects as he sleeps so bewitchingly is very different.

For a start, he's not standing with his feet well apart and a serious, almost swaggering look about him, but is nearly always sitting or lying in his stockinged feet, his expression impenetrable. The pale mask, which he never removes, is held at the back by four knotted ties; it obscures a third of his face and cuts his mouth in half. He no longer wears soldier's clothes and, as far as the child can see, the empty military coat now hanging in the storeroom bears no relation to the austere but small-scale uniform that's so familiar to her.

Léo solemnly shakes her head. She closes her eyes, not to imitate Toussaint, but to remember the sort of father he was to her before.

One day she reaches out a finger till it skims the white mask, but Jeanne stops her – just before, to their terror, the sleeping man opens his eyes, groans and props himself on one elbow.

Toussaint eats little and with extraordinary concentration, infinitely slowly. Only rarely does he sit facing his wife and daughter, when, with the back of her hand, Jeanne shoves aside her flower-making things to clear a small space on the table for a meal. More often than not, he keeps well away, in the shadowy storeroom. He probably wants to avoid showing them what his face looks like when he chews carefully, when he drinks and the edge of the mask rides up. He swallows down his stew in little sips then, and raises his bowl or turns away so that Jeanne and Léo can see nothing of that part of his face.

When Jeanne chances across him one morning putting slivers of bread into his mouth, he opens his jaws so unbearably cautiously that she immediately looks away.

The subject of food, which is already so difficult to get hold of after four years of war, becomes an additional burden hanging between them.

Days go by. Toussaint has been home a week and nothing's happening. He's just there, shut down, shut away.

Jeanne meanwhile is out for between one and three hours every day: she goes to Léo's school, queues outside empty shops, makes deliveries, picks up orders, or simply has a moment's respite with Sidonie, because for practical reasons the seamstress is now the one who keeps her door open.

And Jeanne doesn't know what Toussaint does when she's not there. Who knows; unseen by her, he might be restored to what he was before, a man of flesh and words.

7

It's unimaginable.

These were the opening words that Joseph Caillet used when he came to tell his daughter-in-law about it.

When the old man had arrived at Val-de-Grâce, he'd stood waiting for an hour in a corridor with smells he didn't like and sounds he didn't recognize. People walked past. Some busy, working. Others swaddled in white bandaging, hampered, taking slow steps.

In the end a nurse came and said, I'm responsible for visitors.

This seemed a good thing, so Joseph nodded his head and rolled up his cap in his hands. He was there to see Toussaint Caillet, his son, who'd been hospitalized in Department 5 – Facial Injuries since late December 1916.

He's been with you eighteen months, he felt it worth adding, sombrely.

The nurse – whom Joseph called 'the girl' in his account – showed him to the day room. The girl never stopped smiling, she didn't, and she spoke too much and too quickly. The men in there lay on rows of beds or stood about in groups, clustered by the windows. When he and the nurse entered the room, almost all of them, but not all of them, turned to look.

Toussaint's going to be so pleased to see you, that's what the girl said. She said his name with a peculiar spontaneity, and Joseph felt obscurely stung. What right, what weight of experience could this slip of a stranger lay claim to, what shared history could she be implying?

Oh, his son was going to be so incredibly happy! And what courage these men on Department 5 showed every day!

Joseph scanned the large room to pick out the boy's face, not taking the time or the trouble to look at anything else, but he wasn't there, Toussaint wasn't there.

He'd seen straight away that his son wasn't there. This stupid girl with her know-it-all attitude had misled him.

No, no. Private Caillet, that's who I want to see, he reiterated.

The girl had just shown him to the bedside of a patient, apparently chosen at random. Why this man, who wasn't his son? Joseph had wondered.

His ageing eyes now focused more clearly on the beds and the proliferation of compresses. And then the faces appeared to him. It was just that the wretched girl with her babbling and her fine words had distracted him.

Well, get to know his fellow patients for a start, she trilled in a falsely cheerful voice.

And her surprisingly powerful girl's fingers gripped the muscles of Joseph's arm as if to gauge whether he was made of strong enough stuff, whether he could withstand it.

That lad lying on the bed, Joseph said he'd remember him for the rest of his life. Except his name, he'd forgotten that. Maybe a man with a face like that didn't really have a name anyway.

At this point in his description, Joseph fell silent for a minute, nodding slowly as if concentrating on something. And then he said it again: It's unimaginable.

And Jeanne really did have trouble imagining what he might have seen in Department 5. She couldn't imagine anything.

Joseph just carried on staring, his blue eyes wide open, eyes so like his son's and yet so different. Then he blinked once and snatched a breath loudly through his nose.

Facial injuries, they call it. Soldiers wounded in the face. That's all they have in Department 5. Just that, all over the place.

Jeanne said she knew.

What she didn't know was that the patient to whom old man Caillet had been led – the nurse clutching him by the bicep, smiling and chattering all the while – had surely been one of the most hideously affected.

A hole.

His face, he meant, just a hole.

Parked at the end of the bed with the nurse, Joseph had flinched his head away to avoid falling into that hole, but the man in the bed to the right, whose covers were tucked in up to his neck despite the heat, had one eye punctured and his cheek was turned inside out, the next man had no nose or chin and the one beyond had his arm in a metal contraption, pointing skywards and clamped to the side of his mouth.

And while old man Caillet spun round, not free of these disfigured men and their bandages but at least of the nurse's grip, he found himself confronted with a creature plodding laboriously towards him, his face cleaved open by a crack like a fissure in a chopping block.

This one wanted to talk to him, to Joseph.

You see, he told Jeanne, it was as if – as if I could no longer recognize the human race, as if they were a different species.

Those boys' heads were made of wax, of butter, dotted here and there with crevasses and blinking eyes, or their heads were made of pale oak wood that had been planed all wrong, and Joseph knew what he was talking about, he was a carpenter. A man made of wood, that's what it was, coming towards him to talk, to shake his hand and then lead him off to who knew what sort of nightmare.

This is Monsieur Herry, the girl had said, he was burned by a flare last year.

Joseph couldn't go on. He couldn't describe any more. That bit, about the man in pale oak wood, he probably shouldn't have told her, not Jeanne.

He filled his pipe with grey tobacco, lit it and sucked on it a few times. He pinched the bridge of his nose.

And then kept going.

*

In the middle of Department 5's large main ward the nurse in charge of visitors had finally stopped talking. And when Joseph turned to look at her, choking, doing what he could to bite back his fear, she looked at him appraisingly until he'd calmed down. Then he looked her right in the eye and as soon as he succeeded in standing straight without swaying she nodded.

She must have thought I was ready. I can tell you one thing, my dear – that wasn't completely true.

By the bed of that poor lad whose name he'd forgotten, surrounded by men with appalling facial injuries, the mutilated, the drooling and the disfigured, Joseph felt terribly tense and terribly cold in spite of the stifling weather. But he'd seen enough to withstand the shock to come. The girl led him to a small bedroom set apart from the others, where, standing alone, his son really was waiting for him.

Here Joseph broke off again.

Yes. That's right. Toussaint Caillet was there, cleaned up and alive in that small, separate bedroom.

Well? Jeanne asked.

Well what? Well, yes, he was a bit different, damaged, of course he was, but still, compared to the other buggers he'd seen there, it was nothing at all.

He still had his good eyes, his good looks, she mustn't fret, Jeanne mustn't.

And what did he say?

Ah.

Did he ask about me? Did he want to know?

Yes, the old man said. Oh, yes, Toussaint had been given his fill of news. About her and the little poppet.

Joseph told his son that only the day before he'd had her on his knee, little Léonie, that she was pretty as a picture, bless her. Pretty as a picture, he said that several times. The spitting image of her grandmother.

That particular day, Léo had actually been at Replonges with her maternal grandmother, because Jeanne had sent her there. The food and fresh air in the country always put more weight on her bones than in Paris.

But the fact that Joseph hadn't seen his granddaughter for at least three months didn't matter. Pretty as a picture and good as gold, that was the truth.

Talking to Jeanne, Joseph smiled as he described the child.

And when she asked him what her husband had really said, the old man held his chin in his hand and rubbed it hard, a little too briskly. He pulled on the corners of his moustache.

He hesitated.

Now that he came to think of it, Jeanne, oh dear, goodness, he seemed to think that Toussaint hadn't said anything at all.

8

At the beginning of the war, word was that the country would easily hold out for six weeks, but no one knew what would become of it if this went on for six months.

Word was that the north was a real bloodbath.

Word was people were dying of hunger in Reims.

Word was their cannon had a range of 800 kilometres.

Word was refugees in one village were eating bread mixed with straw.

Word was Joffre would blow up a whole city.

Word was the trenches were almost palatial, there were warm showers and you could settle down in a chair as if at a show.

Word was whole waves of Germans were collapsing one on top of the other.

Word was they cut off children's hands and set fire to adults' clothes.

Word was their shells only caused bruising, their shrapnel phuttered limply and their bullets went through flesh without tearing anything.

Word was, despite Pope Benedict XV's efforts, there'd be no Christmas truce.

Word was there were minimal losses in the French ranks.

Word was there was a hospital for mutilated children in the Indre-et-Loire region.

Word was, as of the fifteenth, they'd be dropping a bomb on Paris every five minutes.

Word was, spring would come around one morning.

9

One evening in early November Jeanne comes home with two proper sealed bottles. When she stopped off at the workshop after delivering Sidonie's aprons, she met the paper dyer, who's been dabbling in the black market since the beginning of the war. Bodin left school in '83 and he likes to make sure everybody knows it. Give or take a few years he could have joined the Territorials, but he dodged everything. He stayed behind, in the calm of the workshop.

Mind you, Jeanne thinks whenever she sees him, the man looks younger and more vigorous than plenty of soldiers on leave seen in their uniforms on the Grands Boulevards and elsewhere in the city. And she can't help but succumb to the same unanswered questions, as she does whenever she meets a man who's stayed behind – the shirkers, the elderly and the misshapen.

What would have happened if Bodin had gone off to war like the rest of them in August 1914? Would he have been assigned to the same regiment as Toussaint? Would they have become friends; would he, Bodin, have had it in him to search selflessly for Private Caillet around the Côte-du-Poivre that day, when he had only just been reported missing by his platoon commander? With his sheer obstinacy, courage and intuition, couldn't he have found him in the mud, under the snow, and lifted him out, and then, braving the cold and enemy bullets, carried him on his back to the first aid station? Who knows whether Bodin with his bright eyes and sturdy limbs wouldn't have found him sooner than the others did, the Thérys, the Montagnons and the Chinese soldiers with their outlandish names, men whom Toussaint used to mention in his letters and who, she imagined, had abandoned him for hours, unconscious, his face smothered in blood and mud, his knees clamped in the jaws of freezing water?

Couldn't he, she dares to think, couldn't he just have been injured instead of Toussaint?

Leaning self-importantly against the door in the dyeing room, his fingers browned by flower pigments rather than mud and blood, Bodin always seems worlds away from imagining such torments.

At the exact moment when Toussaint was hit, Jeanne thinks, the dyer was probably asleep in bed. Or inanely finishing off a snack with a lick of his lips while he dunked Nainsook muslin petals in fuchsine or picric yellow.

In the workshop today, Bodin told her that Serbia had been liberated. He talked about the English, the Americans, the Belgians and the Italians. To see his beaming face, anyone would think he knew them all personally. Those countries and those people. He mentioned the Kaiser, and also asked after Jeanne's husband, but she didn't want to answer, didn't know how to.

All the same, because she'd just been paid for a fortnight's work she took two bottles from him, as well as the bag of sawdust for burning that he'd brought for her, as agreed the previous Wednesday.

Bodin had finished reading his paper so he let her have it; at no extra charge, he added with a little smile.

On her way home, Jeanne was struck by how many people had gathered in groups at crossroads and tram stops, outside cafes and shops, chattering animatedly. She usually paid precious little attention to gawkers, but Bodin's optimism had roused her curiosity. She caught snatches of conversation as she passed.

Parisians were talking about the war more than ever. About the end of the war. Like the dyer at the workshop, some were saying that Kaiser Wilhelm had abdicated and that Serbia had been liberated. They also mentioned the Belgians, the English, the Italians and the Americans.

It gave her quite an appetite.

She bartered for three Rennet apples, with hardly any bruising, from a woman she knew who peddled fruit and vegetables on rue de Cléry. And outside her building, just before climbing the stairs, she spent eight sous on two paper cones filled with hot chips.

Laden with this haul she opens the door, brandishing the provisions and the sawdust for the stove. She's out of breath, and without thinking what she's doing starts whooping: Serbia! Serbia!

Léo jumps to her feet and Toussaint, who's sitting in his armchair, for the first time shows the beginnings of a smile under his mask.

She knows, or rather she senses, that it's neither the liberation of Serbia nor the prospect of a possible armistice that has elicited this rictus.

It's her, Jeanne, it's all down to her. And she knows this because of his eyes, the eyes that have suddenly reappeared in her husband's face. Still hidden by the white mask, his mouth, his cheek and – who knows – his ear weren't the only things injured back there at Côte du Poivre.

Toussaint's eyes. Toussaint's heavenly eyes. They had almost lost all their spark, but Jeanne suddenly recognizes them, as they flash briefly.

His eyes – of a blue that hovers between nigella and chicory – are accentuated by thin longitudinal creases and are open quite wide. She couldn't put into words the effect they have on her, the effect those eyes of his had on her every time they undressed her, burrowed into her and reinvented her. What she can say is that, at least until August 1914, they never failed.

And as she came through the door, she was what brought them back to life.

She, Jeanne.

When making flowers, Jeanne metamorphoses into an incredibly self-possessed creature whose focus, skill and attention to detail enthral anyone who has the opportunity to watch her work. She can make 900 cowslip flowers in a day. Her hands produce improbable tea roses as opulent as lettuces, explosive swells of petals speckled with a shimmer of blood red or cherry red. She conjures up clusters, stalks and ears, umbels and flower heads, all more beautiful and more real than the real thing.

But there's also the other Jeanne, the one who's so slapdash and half-hearted when she does the housework, who bangs into the walls and furniture, who chips plates and glasses, and throws her daughter in the air, her arms thrusting skywards till they're both giddy.

Appearing suddenly in the doorway, all at once she was back, the Jeanne who was all sinew and tendons, with her shopping bag bulging like a belly on her elbow, holding out two hedgehogs of prickly chips, some of which, in the shock of the moment, fell to the floor, and with two black bottles and the rolled-up newspaper awkwardly clamped under the other arm.

It was Jeanne writ large, fully alive. The one who breathlessly cries, Serbia, Serbia, as if this country that neither of them had ever heard of before the war has become precious to them, yoked to their own story.

That woman was Jeanne, and Toussaint smiled at her.

Léo sulks for the rest of the evening. She sulks about the chips, feeling she didn't have her fair share, she sulks because of the acrid smoke produced by the burning sawdust and she sulks because of the wine that her parents drain, one bottle after the other, altering the atmosphere.

Before mobilization, Toussaint had his daily litre of red wine like most factory workers. At the end of a day's work he'd happily supplement it with a small glass of spirits from a wine merchant, in the company of fellow workers. He was a sensible man. Some of the others downed three or four litres on top of their regular bottle of wine, their eau de vie and absinthe.

Jeanne, on the other hand, has always preferred cider or milk, and all in all drinks very little.

Which is why this is the first time that alcohol has crossed the threshold since her husband came home. And she's been wondering whether he missed it, her Toussaint, whether it was usual practice at Val-de-Grâce to give the injured red wine. She hasn't mentioned it. She's just brought home a pack of shag tobacco a couple of times and left it on the sideboard without a word.

But what they have this evening is two sealed bottles of wine.

As usual, Toussaint goes into the storeroom to drink, but after a while he comes out and sits back down in the armchair, more or less facing his wife and daughter, in three-quarter profile, wiping what can be seen of his lips less and less bashfully, with a familiar swipe of the back of his hand.

The dyer's wine isn't good, but it relaxes Jeanne's and Toussaint's shoulders, deadens and softens their movements. The distance between them seems to have shrunk. Old waves are stirring, waves they thought had died. Léo can feel them too, and the child – who's only ever known her mother to be attentive to her alone, apparently fascinated by her small person – is put out.

She holds her tongue, little Léo, scowls into her doll, tries surreptitiously to slip under the eiderdown, where she's no longer allowed to sleep.

The sawdust in the stove is now incubating its embers and swallows back its dull smoke at last. Jeanne is warmed more by the tipple than by the sullen fire and starts reading fragments from the newspaper out loud, parking her lower back against the corner of the sideboard.

She reads, Glorious British Victory, 10,000 Prisoners and 200 Cannon. She reads, The Magnificent Tally of Austrian Defeat.

On the second page, with her eyes hidden as she holds the paper wide open, she then judiciously chooses what can safely be relayed.

She does not read the article about firewood coupons, for which Toussaint's circumstances don't make them eligible, skips over the story about the former maid who now lives a life of furious debauchery since her husband went off to the front, and who recently attacked a woman in the street, striking her fourteen times with a hammer.

She bites heartily into her apple while Toussaint carefully slices his into sufficiently thin slivers to get them gently through the obstacle of his mouth.

She reads the short item about the possible scrapping of the blue sleeves that, in an attempt to avoid bombing raids by the Boche, have covered the city's gaslights for months and months. In the legal pages, she chooses a story about a duel fought with bottles in a wine cellar, and laughs out loud when she gets to the head cellarman's comical demise.

She does not read the obituaries for the fallen and skirts round all the people who can't individually thank everyone who's offered them condolences.

She plucks three preposterous sentences from *A Horrible Drama*, the newspaper's daily serial, and reads out advertisements for Le Tip butter substitute, for concerts at the Théâtre des Champs-Élysées and for the operetta *La Reine Joyeuse*, which is the talk of Paris.

She does not read out Belgian Children Injured by German Machine-Gun Fire.

Straightening slightly, she now reads the whole advertisement for the Extuber Bust Developer, which can help any woman completely transform her chest in a fortnight. She reads, A beautiful bosom is a woman's most exquisite charm. She arches her back, aware that she has no need of the Extuber Bust Developer. Her eyes meet the blue of Toussaint's, he's looking at her intently, looking at her breasts, her waist and her mouth, unblinking.

She swallows hard and doesn't read the Situations Vacant asking for tool-makers turners fitters splicers wheelwrights people with foot and leg injuries for warehouse work jam-makers sheet-metal workers welders and riveters.

Nor does she read Hérial Pills for Weak Men or the special offers about Buying Used Dentures, but, proudly brandishing one of her feet in its celebrated National Shoe, she reads the advertisement offering Pairs of Second-Hand Shoes.

She reads about Ardèche Chestnuts, Saint-Jean-de-Luz Sardines and All's Well That Ends Well Thanks to Pink Pills for Pale People.

And she looks Toussaint square in the eye.

Off to one side, Léo starts grizzling and Jeanne reads Sensational Sales of Bedroom Furniture at Herzog.

Huddled up to her doll, the child finally falls asleep in the double bed, with her head on her mother's pillow. Her nose is blocked and her breathing loud.

Lulled by this whistling sound, they're now alone together. Jeanne has exhausted what diversion and colour the newspaper can offer, and she folds up its pages before abandoning it on the floor. Her hip draws away from the sideboard, she comes closer to Toussaint, who, although he was attentive while she read, hasn't moved a single centimetre, is still anchored in his chair with four pips and the stalk of his apple sitting neatly on one of his knees.

They study each other from closer up. Each smelling the other, the smell of their skin and the wine.

Show me, she starts by saying.

And because, hearing these words, he blinks, making the blue that hovers between nigella and chicory disappear for a brief but agonizing second, she leans forward and speaks more quietly.

Surely you can do it for *me*.

Under his nose, mingled into his short moustache, threads of scarring splay out as fine as insect legs, and Jeanne's urge to touch intensifies.

Yes, his eyes are open again, but Toussaint is serious, motionless, and there's a barely discernible quiver of anxiety along his hairline.

For me, she whispers.

For me, Toussaint.

These cajoling syllables in Jeanne's mouth, from her parted lips that look as if they're readying for a kiss, seem to imply that Toussaint himself is still for her.

For me, Toussaint.

And because he still doesn't respond, a veil falls over her and she stiffens.

Is it that he can't talk? Will he never be able to talk to her again?

When she asks this, Toussaint leans back into the chair, tilts his hips forward and, with his breath gurgling in his throat, reaches into his trouser pocket. From there he produces a folded piece of paper the size of a postcard. He hands it to Jeanne and she, surprised, takes it from him and backs away.

So he's written her a letter.

While she was out on her errands, he did some thinking and scrawled a couple of words to her. Unless he planned this from the start, in anticipation of this very request, which, it has to be said, she hasn't yet ventured to make, or of a gesture that she hasn't yet attempted, and he's had this note there in his pocket, waiting, a message that would explain without speaking.

After her initial astonishment, she retreats to the storeroom. The darkness in there may not help with reading, but it strikes her as a possible shelter, away from the nigella eyes.

There are only two words to read.

'NOT YET' is all he's written, in the middle of the unfolded piece of paper. She can turn it this way and that and tilt it towards the light all she likes, there's nothing more to be gained than this ceasefire.

Not yet what? Not yet who? She doesn't understand. Hasn't she waited long enough, with the 1,554 days that this war's been going on, and the seven that he's been home, drawing out the strangest week she's ever lived, with him but without him, the two of them – Jeanne and Léo – crushed by his mask and his silent eyes, hasn't she been patient enough?

She storms out of the storeroom and, in a combination of fury and disappointment, reproduces the gesture that Léo began a few days earlier, reaching one extended finger towards the square of white cotton.

She needs to know.

If he's as hideous as all that, if she's married to one of the monsters that old man Caillet described from his visit to Department 5, if there's nothing human left behind that white mask, well, then she at least has a right to see, to know. If she's got to get used to it, she might as well start this evening.

But Toussaint throws himself against the back of the chair, screwing up his eyes, and their blue disappears between his lids, as if, even from a distance, Jeanne's hand has scorched his irises. And just as she clenches her teeth and, in spite of everything, prepares to move the mask aside with the tips of her fingers, there's a loud explosion of sound behind her, accompanied by a rush of cold air.

Léo sits up in bed and shrieks.

When Jeanne turns round, Sidonie is there by the door, God knows how she managed to open it – Sidonie rooted on the spot, her hair awry and her red face looking disturbingly contracted as it looms out of the darkness on the landing.

Toussaint seems to press himself harder still against the faded calico of the chair, as if trying to burrow his chest inside it, while Jeanne slowly drops her hand.

10

Sidonie has been married twice and has had five sons.

Jean Herbin, known as Nono, who was employed at a printing works, was her first husband. Cowardly, ill-tempered and keen on his drink, Nono died a year after the birth of his only son, Eugène.

Sidonie then set up home with a placid metalworker by the name of Albert Buche, whom she met at a dance in July 1899. A year later André was born, then Ernest and the child only ever known by the nickname Zizi. René came last, less than two years before his father died.

Zizi went in just one night. He was five months old. André died when he was three. René lived five and a half summers, Ernest eight.

This was before the war. Ernest's death in October 1913 was the last in this devastating succession. All that Sidonie had to pamper on her knee was Bobi, the old ginger tom. There were no children left.

Eugène, meanwhile, was still a butcher's apprentice on rue Thorel. He was sixteen. He was almost a man and he was alive.

At the time, the Caillets were living on rue des Cascades

in the 20th arrondissement. Jeanne and Sidonie didn't even know each other. And yet, without realizing it, the two women already had something in common, because a few months before René and Ernest died Jeanne's first daughter, snuggled against her father's side, had stopped breathing.

For days Jeanne had crouched at the foot of the cot listening to the child's lungs painfully expanding and deflating.

Bella had just turned two. As her alveoli contracted under her thin cotton nightdress, they made a sound like silky tissue paper, the rustle of organdie being crumpled, the selfsame delicate organdie that Jeanne used for her roses, and that she need only roll over a heated ball to make them bloom in a perfect, smooth curve.

Bella's lungs may have been made of silk but her mother had never laid eyes on a more translucent, wilting flower. This one, this fragile bloom, she didn't know how to handle. Her hands and her flower-maker's tools were as little use to her as her rocking and singing, her kisses and even her prayers. With the passing days, the huge-eyed flower shrivelled irretrievably while Jeanne's belly was secretly already carrying the tiny seed that would be Léo.

In the space of fourteen years, Jean, Albert, André, Ernest, Zizi, René and Bella had left more or less suddenly, but all defeated by the same ailment. With Jean, the first husband, they called it consumption, but Jean's consumption was the same tuberculosis that took the others.

*

Sidonie was left with only her eldest son.

He was in the class of 1917. With his pig-headedness, his swaggering ways and his sturdy, vigorous body always on the move, Eugène was the Herbin-Buche family's miracle survivor. When conscription was announced on the first day of August 1914, it may well have been this weighty privilege that drove the young apprentice to enlist with the French troops earlier than expected.

By getting away from Paris and gaining access to what he thought of as men's adventures, he was escaping his mother's oppressive fears. And after all, if he'd survived Koch's bacillus, he'd stand up to the Boche just as easily.

Eugène wrote to rue de la Lune from time to time. Brief cards that Sidonie showed straight to Jeanne, comparing them with Toussaint's, which were more frequent and more tender but equally vague on the realities of what the men were enduring at the front.

And working from the scant clues apportioned to them, the two women dreamed up an imaginary geography of France, a shifting, hazy, comforting landscape. Maissin, Maisons-Noires, Soissons, Tahure, Bois-Bouchet... names that they repeated to themselves through the day as they toiled over their work, saying them again and again in their heads and sometimes out loud, until they came to be paired with naive images, hushed, clean of any blood, hardly even dotted with barbed wire or mired in mud, a sort of bucolic scene surrounded by thickets, with rivers running through it, scattered with a gossamer powdering of snow or thousands of dandelions.

If Eugène happened to mention the terrible thirst that tormented him in June 1916, Sidonie immediately assuaged her son's suffering – and her own from reading about it – by picturing the teenager lying beside a stream with his face in its cool water as he took great draughts of it. She was light years away from imagining what the young infantryman hadn't been able to admit, at least not to her: that he and the others in his squadron who'd survived had to resort to chewing on roots, sucking any dirty fluid found in the bottom of helmets abandoned by the dead, and burning the roofs of their mouths as they closed their eyes and took little sips of their own urine.

The clear current of Sidonie's stream soothed her as she tirelessly made drawstring bags and apron strings, topstitched cartloads of absorbent fabric to make sanitary towels or stitched the seams of rabbit-skin mittens for soldiers other than her son.

Their two worlds.

Full of affection and pain, and perfectly impermeable to each other.

That second autumn Toussaint had written, Say hello to Eugène, tell him to stay strong, and Sidonie, suddenly invested with a real message, a task, had swiftly passed on the older man's good wishes, adding to them a pair of socks, five francs arduously saved up and an artificial forget-me-not from Jeanne.

Eugène and Toussaint had crossed paths only once, when they happened to be on leave at the same time the previous spring. So they didn't know each other well, but that was enough to exchange a kind word and for the two women to concoct new ties.

And as soon as a letter arrived, Sidonie or Jeanne could breathe easily for a few hours. Their soldiers, connected to each other by invisible strings, were still alive.

And the two women with them.

Then, in the spring of 1917, while Toussaint's brief but regular letters continued to be sent from Val-de-Grâce, Eugène's stopped dead.

At first Sidonie was rational. She tried to be, in any event, and this kept her going for three weeks. Jeanne, Mother Birot, the butcher and anyone else with whom she discussed it did their best to convince her that the vagaries of the postal system or even, if Eugène was too careless, the likelihood of censorship could explain this delay in mail.

Come on, surely Sidonie remembered that autumn when she got only one card? There was nothing to worry about with Eugène. Eugène could survive the worst, nothing could happen to him.

But the dam eventually broke. Out on the street, if she saw a wet pigeon ruffling its feathers at the edge of a gutter, a jostled child tumble on the paving stones or a group of high-spirited soldiers on leave, Sidonie would start to cry and would be quite unable to stop.

However fiercely she tried to recruit her imagination, the old images of cool streams and hot meals collapsed inside her head, now interspersed with explosions and bayonets that steamrollered her night after night. If tuberculosis could go by the name of consumption, couldn't it just as easily assume the name, the faces and the cannon of the Boche?

Even so. Without admitting it to herself, of course she still harboured the hope that somewhere far away, somewhere safe, her miracle survivor was still alive.

Eugène was tough. Insolent and impatient at times. Surely her friends were right then; there were people who were trying to silence him. Couldn't Eugène simply be suffering the vengeful anger of some mail officer who'd decided to stop sending his letters? Or, with time on his hands, couldn't he have been lured by a peasant girl's pretty face and taken temporary refuge in a nearby farm, or been taken prisoner by the Germans, or even, too bad, have deserted?

Sidonie continued to send letters to her son for months, writing three times a week until the summer of 1918. She never received a word in reply. She also wrote to his corporal, his sergeant, his lieutenant and his platoon commander. What had happened? What had they done with Private Herbin, what had they done with her only child, her whole family?

She wept, she begged, she threatened. And if she'd had their addresses, she would also have written to the Virgin Mary, the archbishop and the Pope, to whom she prayed every morning at Our Lady of Good News and at all hours of the day deep inside her belly.

In the end, at about six o'clock on the evening of 5 November, the local Special Messenger Service walked up rue de la Lune and the three women introduced themselves to the caretaker, asking to see widow Herbin.

Sidonie was known by her second husband's name so there was a moment of confusion, which was soon cleared up when the first name was mentioned. Widow Herbin was in fact widow Buche, but there was only one Eugène in the whole building.

Herbin, Eugène Jules Emile. That is your son's name, isn't it? came the honeyed voice from the dark landing.

A smiling Sidonie, with her fingers still on the door handle, came face to face with three ghosts. On the floors below, inquisitive doors opened and closed with varying degrees of discretion.

The Special Messenger Service.

People would look out for them from their windows and on the streets, these bearers of death wearing black clothes and gloves, war widows themselves, paid three francs by the town hall to come in person and – with all the appropriate compassion and patriotic fervour – announce the deaths of fathers, brothers, husbands and sons.

The French military authorities had finally tracked down the miracle survivor.

*

Sidonie gave no reply. Hearing those three names, she could offer no confirmation. She simply stood aside to let the women in, and the oldest of the three closed the door softly.

Eugène had fallen on the Chemin des Dames in May 1917, eighteen months earlier. This exactly matched the time when his letters had stopped, and Sidonie nodded grimly.

They didn't know whether the boy had been alone at the fateful moment, whether he'd been felled on the spot or had taken days to die, they couldn't say what had happened to his body, whether it had remained intact, whether, somewhere, he'd been given any kind of grave.

To date, none of this information had been supplied. But she mustn't lose hope. The details might emerge later.

As for them, these members of the Special Messenger Service, they were just here to say that Private Herbin was no longer alive. Broken-hearted, they offered his mother the condolences of an entire, deeply sorry nation.

What matters is knowing your child died a hero, murmured one of them. And thanks to him France is on the brink of victory.

Eugène Herbin, who died courageously at the age of twenty.

Eugène Herbin, son of France. He's at rest, *madame*, asleep.

My, isn't your son handsome, Madame Herbin, isn't your soldier handsome and isn't he tall?

The youngest of the women, with a ruddy complexion and pitted skin, tilted her cheek towards her shoulder and reached out an arm with a pained smile.

Sidonie didn't move.

She didn't ask any questions. She didn't howl, didn't keen. Didn't even open her mouth. Her arms stayed limply by her sides, her eyes dry.

And when it finally occurred to her that these three women had finished what they had to say, she nodded, turned around and went back to sit at her sewing machine. Once there, she drew the lamp closer, picked up the apron string she'd been working on before they arrived and started operating the treadle with both feet, not paying the women any further attention.

It goes without saying that during the course of its painful assignments the Special Messenger Service had witnessed a vast array of reactions, from the most vehement denials to utterly despairing acceptance. But this one, which amounted to a sort of stupor bordering on mental derangement, was unnerving to say the least.

A hand laid a piece of paper on the edge of Sidonie's cluttered table, then the three women in black furtively conferred with only their eyes before scuttling away, muttering.

She was lucky, the seamstress was lucky: the ceremony would take place the very next day at nine o'clock sharp.

It is this piece of paper that Sidonie is holding when, scarlet-faced and disorientated, she barges into the Caillets' home a few hours later.

When she has recovered from the shock of Sidonie's sudden entrance and the silence that the poor woman offers to her two equally baffled neighbours, Jeanne takes the notification and starts to read it.

There it is in writing: certificates will be handed out at a ceremony at the town hall the next morning.

Jeanne doesn't think. She doesn't know what this means exactly, so she just says what she has to say.

She'll be there. She'll go with Sidonie. They'll go together.

A certificate. Neither the Herbins nor the Buches have a clear idea what one of those is. And anyway, Sidonie's no longer in a fit state to imagine, speculate, explain or even – by the looks of her – think anything at all. Still full of words, actions, tears and exclamations only yesterday, the seamstress has vacated her body. She doesn't cry, doesn't say a word. She's just a puppet, as inert as Léo's rag doll.

When Mother Birot, tipped off by Jeanne, comes to knock at Sidonie's door a little later, Sidonie doesn't answer. An ear pressed up against the door picks up nothing but the regular rocking of the sewing machine's treadle. And because the camouflage factory that employed Mother Birot for three years has dismissed its workers for want of soldiers, the old woman can't afford the luxury of letting down the workroom that took her on a few months ago.

The seamstress will understand that she can't come with her to this mysterious certificate ceremony.

Jeanne alone will go with Sidonie.

11

As the two women walk haltingly through the streets, the one escorting the other, people around them carry on with their lives and continue with their conversations. Everybody's mouths are full of the same names, proliferated thrillingly by the imminent end of the conflict.

But Jeanne and Sidonie have stopped listening, stopped looking.

With a furrowed brow, Jeanne keeps a constant eye open, in case Sidonie goes and slips as she steps off a pavement, collapses in a heap in the road or blunders into someone. She talks to her all the way, and her words are meaningless, they're just a long ribbon of butterflies with truncated wings, a ribbon unspooling around them in an attempt to distract them.

She mustn't catch cold, they're going to be there on time, this shoe, this National Shoe, it doesn't half hurt, the beggar, anyone would think they'd wedged a pebble between the layers of the sole, and how about Sidonie, are her ankle boots comfortable, if only they could get hold of a good hunk of chuck steak, or half a chicken, if only, one of these days, they could be given just a bit of a let-up at the workshop or the department store, if only Spanish flu, if only they were on time.

Some sixty of them are gathered in the large hall used for weddings, mostly women, every one of them dressed in black, solemn-faced, along with young children in their Sunday best, an amputee in his uniform and medals, and a dozen or so tearful elderly people leaning on their walking sticks. These are the Families of Soldiers Killed by the Enemy, and although she is not, strictly speaking, one of their number, Jeanne feels more at home here than the woman she brought with her.

Up on a rostrum, flanked by his deputies, the mayor with his tricolour sash over his barrel chest gives an interminable speech, and there's a pomposity in his voice and his words for which they are quite unprepared.

Standing next to Jeanne, Sidonie seems lost – she glances from left to right, her stunned eyes gradually growing dim. Jeanne holds her firmly, and the more the mayor's sentences sprawl and tie themselves in knots across their imagined landscape, the more she convulsively tightens her grip around the flesh of Sidonie's forearm, unaware that she is doing it.

The mayor's words are incomprehensible, they come and go and sting. Jeanne doesn't know whether it's up to them, the women here, these workwomen, to tame the words and arrange them in the correct order, whether it's really to them that they're addressed. They flow too quickly. They fly too high. There are too many of them.

Thunder and fire, men freezing and caked in mud and half poisoned by noxious gases, heroes, brothers, love, defeat, hope, victory, history, peace, blood, martyrs, children. His speech is riddled with these impassioned fragments. And, just like the battles experienced by those who are now dead, these official words accumulate terrifyingly, chaotically over the gathering. It's a bombardment, and Jeanne, busy as she is shoring up her neighbour's faltering frame, struggles to withstand its fire for more than a few minutes.

Every one of you – man, woman and child – knows that this war is about to end in glorious victory, is a work of such towering beauty that it justifies every sacrifice... No, they're not completely dead, these men who were so humble in their day-to-day lives and who, in the heat of battle, stood so tall!

While scattered pockets of the audience ostentatiously sob or brandish laurel leaves, Jeanne can't help her mind drifting back to rue de la Lune. So tall? Just how tall can Toussaint stand now? Toussaint who used to be head and shoulders above most of the others in the tide of workmen spilling from the factory on rue Pixérécourt. It's true that when he was framed before her, the evening he came home, she thought he'd grown taller. But now she's not so sure.

The mayor casts an eye over his notes and continues with quotes from soldiers' letters.

Don't shed too many tears for me, because my death is prized above all others. Let me rest where combat chanced to leave me, surrounded by others who died for France. I'll sleep well there. I'm dying, but I'm dying happy. *Vive la France!*

A deputy takes over now, summoning each of the families in turn to receive their all-important certificate, which the mayor hands to them after much hugging, hand-shaking and tear-filled whispering.

When the name Eugène Herbin rings out across the wedding room, Jeanne tenses painfully, but Sidonie, still clutched by her friend's hand, barely even shudders, merely shifting her face a few centimetres towards the voice as if, recognizing a vaguely familiar sound, she realizes she has been caught daydreaming. And then, just as quickly, her shoulders slump and she sinks back into her torpor.

The silence drags on, here and there a head swivels round, people blow their noses and murmurings gradually build in the crowd of black.

Jeanne steps towards the rostrum. Her eyes are full of tears and bulging with anger, she's shaking and keeps her head lowered. There are actually quite a number of them heading for the stage, because it's not only Sidonie whom Jeanne's half carrying in her arms: she's also taking the lost Eugène, Toussaint's damaged body and the fragile little girl who claims to have two daddies, the one in the photograph and the one who's here, sometimes standing, sometimes lying down, but whose face always hurts.

The men. Eugène and Toussaint.

Half dead. With no known grave.

The women. Sidonie, Jeanne and Léo.

Neither widowed nor orphaned by the war, but still half dead for being alive, for having lost so much. And they, the three of them, these nameless women, have no body over which to weep.

The mayor pats Sidonie's back and slips her the Pro Patria Mori certificate, with all its wings, lances and raised hands. Jeanne thanks him with a quick nod as more grieving people come up behind them.

Just as wealthy dynasties have portraits of their illustrious ancestors, the mayor concludes, brandishing one hand towards the heavens, this certificate which honours the families of soldiers killed by the enemy grants you, my friends, your own nobility. These certificates will be your parchments, sacred relics that you will hang on the walls of your living rooms… Each of you now has your own great ancestor! But remember that if this ancestor raises you above the ranks of others, it behoves you to rise just as high yourselves. For soon your names will shine resplendently from public monuments everywhere, carved in gold letters on slabs of marble. And then you shall hear your dear departed cry: Oh, my family, weep not for me, for I have had the finest death in the world.

12

It's been dark for a long time now.

Léo eventually fell asleep in her cot, and is whistling on each outward breath. Jeanne and Toussaint lie inert, side by side in the double bed, not touching.

The stove snores feebly. Jeanne's whole body is cold and there's a dull ache in her left foot where it was pinched by her tight-fitting, badly made National Shoe.

To think how glad she was to get her hands on a new pair of these shoes! Widespread poverty and the prevailing prices were so incompatible that the government recently decided to launch this much-publicized idea of National Shoes, with monitored manufacturing and a fixed price. The moment they came on the market people swooped on them. Mother Birot claims to have tried twenty shops all across Paris without finding her size. At the end of the summer Jeanne managed to buy a pair from a rose-seller at the workshop. The girl was prepared to hand them over for twenty sous less than their original price, because they'd turned out to be too small for her. But now, with this ache, Jeanne wonders whether it was more than a question of size.

She ought to show them to Toussaint. He would turn them this way and that, feel them and slip his knowing thumbs into strategic places. Like a doctor examining a patient, the former shoe factory worker would find the flaw in a matter of seconds, if there was one.

But she doesn't say anything about her shoe or her pain. The day's been difficult enough. She's had to work late to catch up, and her shoulders, fingers and eyelids seethe with tiny white flashes.

It's around two o'clock in the morning.

She's thinking about Sidonie, strains her ears to catch sounds through the wall. There's complete silence. She wonders whether the seamstress has managed to get to sleep next door, or if, like her, she's just lying on her back in the dark with her eyes wide open and her arms crossed over her chest in an attempt to stay warm. She wonders whether she's managed to cry at last, to cry properly, on her own.

On their way home from the town hall after the certificate ceremony, the two women made a detour to the soup kitchen, but there were so many people there and Sidonie was behaving so oddly that Jeanne had to give up. They headed slowly for rue de la Lune, with the flower-maker still in charge and vigilant.

Once they'd climbed the stairs Jeanne realized that she would have to open her neighbour's door, because Sidonie – standing placidly on the landing with her legs slightly apart – didn't seem to know what she was supposed to be doing. Clutching the large paper rectangle of her certificate, she gazed at Jeanne with a disorientated smile on her lips.

Almost embarrassed, Jeanne opened her mouth, then cleared her throat and nodded. All right then. She said her name, she said, Sidonie, Sidonie, she said, What have they done to you? and then she sighed through her nose and said, We're here, we need the key, we need the key, Sidonie. But she had to rummage through Sidonie's pockets, open the door and steer her inside.

The seamstress's frugal lodging is almost cut off from the world, because the round window intended to illuminate it is so small and murky. The first room serves as a bedroom, sewing workshop and kitchen. The second, which is carefully kept hidden behind a closed door, is Eugène's; in their day, his four brothers had also had their beds and belongings in there.

They went inside; the air was freezing. The little window had been left wide open. Jeanne hurried over and closed it, which wasn't easy because the wooden casement was distorted by years of damp. When she turned round, she realized that the floor and furniture were covered with white linen.

After twenty-seven years in the business, the seamstress had made a speciality of work aprons, for both menservants and chambermaids, and by the looks of it her entire output from the last few days, along with a few pieces waiting to be stitched together, was spread all over the room. Not as if, in a fit of despair after the Special Messenger Service had visited, she'd flung the fabric in the air in a gesture of denial, but rather as if, true to the peculiar calm she'd demonstrated since then, this proliferation obeyed a precise logic. Streams of white over the chest, flounced shapes on the backs of chairs, ghosts hanging from the mirror and the large crucifix over her bed, bandaging tied to the window handle and, to complete the effect, pale pools dotted over the dusty floorboards.

Frozen to the core and feeling a little uncomfortable, Jeanne started tapping her foot on the floor.

Working quickly, she gathered up the more accessible pieces of fabric, folded them perfunctorily and put them over the arm of a chair. She sat Sidonie down. She found three sprouting potatoes and a turnip still steeped in their cooking water in the stew pot. She drained, peeled and cut them into pieces, and they ate them cold at a corner of the table, with some bread.

And while the two women sat chewing slowly together, their cold fingers clumsy, Sidonie's foot beat out a barely perceptible rhythm and her chest flickered with little twitches as if she were full of imprisoned cadences and was beating in time with them.

Through the wall someone could be heard clearing his throat: Toussaint getting up and walking about the room, in the grip of an uncontrollable coughing fit.

Sidonie gave no reaction.

Jeanne would have liked to talk to her about Eugène; this was probably the moment, but what could she possibly say? She'd hardly known the boy, catching only brief glimpses of him when he was on leave. And then what? What pleasures, what future could a woman lay claim to when she'd lost seven men one after the other? What could she, Jeanne, say to a mother who, to make things worse, would never have a coffin? How would she go about it?

Perhaps at the town hall, with all their pontificating verve, they'd taken the only feasible route, after all: they'd ululated ecstatically in memory of these heroes; they'd forbidden tears, and Sidonie had obeyed.

Eugène was the last, the one she'd believed in, the only one who hadn't left her on her own, a lone, guilty survivor.

Eugène! Yes, to her Eugène was now All men.

What could Jeanne have added, with her own semi-tragedy – what placating promises, what lies? Toussaint, by contrast, would eventually heal, would get used to it, settle and pull himself together; at least, she could try to believe this and picture herself coming to terms with the man he'd turned into, with his injury and his memories. And there was Léo too.

But what about Sidonie?

Jeanne watched her chomping on her crust of bread with her head tilted to one side, like a cat. She noticed her grey cheeks, her lips dotted with flakes of dry skin, the dark little blazes of hair escaping from her bun. She saw her empty eyes with their milky coating.

Sidonie?

The seamstress raised her chin, slowly. Their eyes met for just a second and, feeling helpless, incapable of reading what she saw in those eyes, Jeanne instinctively got up from her chair and went to stand behind Sidonie with her hands on her shoulders. She took a deep breath and stayed there, motionless.

Eugène.

She wondered if, in his last moment, he'd finally managed to speak. Had the boy called for his mother before going?

Having experienced it herself months ago, when she received news of Toussaint's injury, she guessed that, deep inside Sidonie's flesh, her boy came back to die a thousand times a day. And that she'd imagined everything. Every position: on his back, on his side, on his stomach or sitting, with his face in the grass or strung up on barbed wire, in the mud of the trenches, in silt or sludge, in his dugout, or even in the stream where she'd pictured Eugène going to quench his thirst. During the day or at night. Sunshine or rain. Every one of his wounds.

She knew that the poor woman had conjured up every type of death throes, intestines, brains, arms or legs ripped out, backs splayed open and eyes punctured. The flies, the maggots and the rats.

Then they came out of nowhere. The tears.

Sidonie simply sat there, upright and stark, while Jeanne, standing behind her, let her tears flow for her.

Minutes passed. Very gradually, Sidonie surrendered at last, resting the back of her head against Jeanne. There was still nearly the same silence, barely disturbed by stifled sobs and sniffing, but, tellingly, something rose from one woman to the other, something more gentle than words: Sidonie's tears, travelling through Jeanne's body and spilling hotly over her cheeks.

In the end Jeanne took a hanky from her sleeve and blew her nose, with a loud noise that marked the end of the downpour.

Sidonie took the last hunk of bread from the table and stuffed it into her mouth, before getting up almost brusquely. She glanced over towards the certificate, which, when she'd come in, she'd put carefully on a shelf in her wardrobe, whose doors hung open.

Then, mumbling incomprehensible syllables, droning a tuneless, wordless song, she plucked a white bib from a chair and some flouncing from the armchair and sat down at her sewing machine, facing the window.

They were going back to work, both of them.

With all that had happened, Jeanne had a good four hours' worth to catch up on. She felt all red and tired. Crying had warmed her, softened her. She awkwardly kissed Sidonie's hair, promised to come back and went home to her ranunculuses.

And now silence has returned to the other side of the wall.

13

The opening is closed with two catgut stitches, turning the edges inwards to limit the loss of mucous surfaces.

A dozen stamens are attached to the tip of a vine stalk and then bound round with thread to form a broomstick shape.

In two separate incisions, one on the inside, the other outside, the edges of the aperture and the whole fibrous mass are excised.

Hyacinths come in soft, subdued colours: blue, mauve, pinkish and red are achieved from rinses with varying concentrations of lapis lazuli, crimson lake, magenta lake or carmine.

Using a buttonhole incision made in the cheek, a scalpel is introduced flatways from front to back under the integument, and the blade is drawn back deep inside.

The colour is made to fade, sometimes towards the tips of the petals, sometimes towards the stem, to achieve a wide variety of nuances.

The small wound that facilitated the insertion of the scalpel is closed with two fine sutures in silkworm gut.

The upper tip of the petals is curled using pliers, while

the bases are rolled over heated balls on a cushion or a square of rubber.

The red edges along the sides of the cut are removed and formed into two small strips, and these are drawn downwards and fixed together.

When the calyxes are to be kept closed, they are spread out over lightly absorbent paper and, once they're needed, skewered with a pin before being attached.

One suture successfully draws together the mauled surfaces, another secures the two strips tightly together.

A second calyx, with five points or claws, also needs to be made and dyed, then rolled into a cone shape to form the base of the corolla.

Using a buttonhole aperture created between the eyebrows, a splint of costal cartilage, taken from the patient himself, is inserted under the integument of the forehead.

The petals are steeped in Ophelia, thinned with water and alcohol. They are striped, stippled and variegated using a sable brush, then rolled, curled and finally assembled onto the stalk to create the most exquisite flower that ever graced a woman's hat.

Our man is now in good shape and can leave Val-de-Grâce to rejoin his unit.

14

And now Jeanne's lying in bed with her eyes open, sensing Toussaint's breath and his sleeping form next to her.

She came to bed without taking the trouble to undo her plaits. They form a dense lump under her head and she tries to nestle it deep into her pillow.

Predictably, she hasn't completely caught up on the outstanding work, even though she stayed up so late that first the sounds in the stairwell and then those in the street fell silent, one by one.

A chance to close her eyes, to sleep.

She'll have to get up early. The darkness outside will still be the same night. Because of what happened to Sidonie, she'll have half a gross of ranunculuses as well as her chores to get through tomorrow.

She must give it time to melt away. In the crook of her plaited bun, her thoughts will go round in circles and then, gradually becoming more compliant, seep like warm oil through her hair, the pillow's feathers and the old wool of the mattress. Her swirling thoughts will finally make way for sleep.

But her thoughts aren't compliant. They keep swirling. Toussaint.

Toussaint, and now Sidonie. Their silence.

Who knows, Léonie might soon come up with the idea of walling herself up inside her head too, never to speak again.

A wordless world seems to be settling around Jeanne. The battles of these last few years have made her neither a widow nor even – and in the dark she tries to find the epithet that doesn't exist – a mother orphaned by her child. No. The war can strike in other ways. The war can rob people of speech.

She pulls the sheet right up to her hairline, swivels her head. The breathing next to her seems to register a slight skip. Toussaint isn't asleep. She shifts a few centimetres, moves slowly closer and stops only when she's right next to him and finds, through the fabric that separates them, the beginnings of his warmth and his attentive breathing.

She takes a deep breath. Sniffs. There's that characteristic smell, that taste at the back of her mouth. She doesn't know whether she's got used to Toussaint's new smell or, from coming into contact with her and his old bed, he's gradually reclaimed his smell from before, the familiar one, a strong smell of salt and leather, smoke and horsehair.

Toussaint is alert to her in the dark.

Almost two years ago now he wrote to say that he wanted her not to come. Yesterday he had said 'Not yet'.

What about her, then?

Her, Jeanne.

*

She whispers in the protective darkness. Whispers under the sheet.

Toussaint.

She says Toussaint, she says it once, then says it again. She's not calling him. She's just saying his name, allowing one syllable and then the other to roll over her face. Despite her exhaustion and fear, her voice is clear, it holds its own.

Toussaint.

And then, as she experiences the same soothing feeling that follows on from that word whenever it comes to her, in that morsel of silence that is still Toussaint, a quiver runs through her. Somewhere inside her it's back, rekindled, the pleasure that seemed to have been lost, the pleasure of holding Toussaint's name in her mouth.

At the beginning of their relationship, and even long after, she often spoke his name to herself, saying it out loud as if diving into the delights of mysterious waters full of aquatic plants. Toussaint. She would offer it to herself in secret, sitting at her table, her solitude disrupted by flowers, or into the wind on the street, his name mingling with the air. Sometimes it made her stumble, stifled by it, drunk on the sound and blushing.

Toussaint, Toussaint and Toussaint again, greedier and greedier for the soft touch of it, a word invented to draw her lips forward, pouting, a word dusted with fine peach fuzz, coiling into her ears and her hair, on her skin.

Toussaint.

Jeanne remembers, launches it into the darkness of the bedroom once more. Toussaint.

And then, carried away, she follows her momentum.

She tells him all about Sidonie. Tells him that, earlier, she had shed Sidonie's first tears.

She also tells him that she's kept every one of the letters he wrote to her in the iron box, every one of the dried flowers and leaves that he sent her, the buttercup, clover leaf, hop, daisy, blueweed and white clover. As for the aluminium ring that he took from a German rifle and engraved with their initials for her, she kept it on her middle finger until last January, until that infamous first letter from Val-de-Grâce. She says that eleven times he started or ended his letters with 'my little darling'. She says she struggled to count all those in which he kissed her or caressed her without saying so. She says that, deep in his trench, he too couldn't have calculated all the times that she took him in her arms, that she held him to her with all her strength.

The words come to her like a rising sweat. And in the darkness they expect no reply.

They tell the story.

She says that after Bella died, two or three days after her burial, she followed him, Toussaint, through the streets, zigzagging across Belleville. And then, all at once, she saw him, Toussaint, slumped against a wall on rue Ramponeau, and from behind she'd watched him crumple and fall, awash with tears, and she, she meanwhile, she'd hung back on the pavement opposite, stunned, unable to go to him, not knowing how to.

She says that Léo had chickenpox one winter, and she caught it straight afterwards. It was the busiest time at the workshop. In spite of the war there was a scrum for flowers. The previous competition from Germany had been swept aside; they still sent them to America, and a few to England, and the manageress had no intention of being kept waiting. Even a qualified worker couldn't slacken for more than a day. No one would wait for her. Things had to be delivered on time. So good-natured Sidonie had done the evening deliveries for her.

She says that one night she battled on making her camellias with such a fever spinning in her head that the almost black petals on her table curled up magically and the vine stalks coiled themselves, transforming into feathery seed heads.

She says that at the school on rue Fondary where, between the ages of thirteen and sixteen, she had been taught the craft of making naturals, she had learned the language of flowers. She says those lists came back to her when she received his letters. Clover – which he sent her twice, in the form of dried leaves and a flower – she remembered meant doubt, buttercups mockery and daisies innocence.

She says that one Sunday in March a shell from Big Bertha fell nearby, a few houses away, at the end of rue de la Lune.

Two people were killed and eight injured that morning. She didn't know any of them but the sound of that explosion had stayed inside her belly like a living animal for months. The detonation lived inside her, it moved about, was made of bones and teeth, and colossal lungs, it opened up holes as big as those she'd seen on the fourth and fifth floors of that building. From then on, with every distant bomb, even any loud noise, it exploded inside her. In the cellar, where she eventually took refuge with the other people from the building several times a week, she tried to reassure Léo. She explained that there was nothing to be afraid of. They were safe, the two of them, nothing would happen to them. And in one sense she wasn't lying. She genuinely believed it. Her body, on the other hand, sang a different tune. Ever since that March morning her body had been made of big slabs of fear.

At this point, Jeanne breaks off and pushes the sheet aside a little. She thinks about what it might have been like for Toussaint, there. She contemplates his man's fear. She wonders whether, before one of them came and stopped the noise once and for all by tearing up his face, Toussaint's frame had been big enough to accommodate the boom of all those bombs.

She says she was frightened for him. And at night, in her fierce efforts to keep him alive, she enlisted the help of familiar images of his face and hands; she wanted to have all of him, moving, before her eyes. Sometimes she lost him, he slipped out of reach, grew so indistinct that she had to fumble her way out of bed, light the lamp and go over to the photograph on the wall.

She also says – very quickly – that when he was in hospital, a week after he arrived there, she broke three eggs into the pan for her supper with Léo. She says that the last egg was full of blood. She says that she stood there over the stove, turned to stone, watching that egg cook in all its blood with the other two, and it was the most violent thing she'd seen in her life because she knew that blood was Toussaint's.

She says that she received the letter the next day. He wanted her not to come.

She says that a little later, in February, she went to Val-de-Grâce with the fierce idea in her belly that she would find him and bring him home, but in the end she didn't have it in her even to get past the front door. It must have been because of the cold.

She says the cold can freeze our impulses.

And then to calm herself, because she must get to sleep, she just says Toussaint twice more for her own benefit.

Toussaint.

Toussaint.

Léo turns over in her cot, grumbling. Jeanne's been talking too loudly.

She closes her eyes.

*

She's so tired. Wavering images of ranunculuses appear. She sighs. She feels a little warmer, her foot hurts a little less. She licks her lips.

And smiles in the dark.

This Jeanne hasn't said, she hasn't asked. Perhaps she's only thought it.

What if from this day forward – now that Serbia's been liberated, the Kaiser's abdicated and the Boche are retreating – she lives surrounded by rocks and walls, what if neither her neighbour nor the man she married ever speaks to her again.

She hasn't said it. She's just beginning to fall asleep.

But next to her, even though she can't see them, she can feel Toussaint's fists clenching, and then all his muscles tensing under the eiderdown. She has just enough time to widen her eyes and barely enough to be afraid.

A word lunges into the darkness. Water springing from a rock. A word of lava and flint, an underwater shard that has rubbed up against saliva and blood, splinters and caves.

He says *no*.

He says no perhaps ten times, and ten times over it's as if Toussaint is angrily thumping his own mouth.

15

The next day is a Thursday. Léo doesn't go to school on Thursdays. She spends the whole day trailing round in circles between the beds and the storeroom, peering – though not venturing her fingers – into the boxes full of the copious ranunculuses Jeanne has just finished making. Then, as she often does, she lays out her own collection of petals and feathers on the tiled floor.

Ever since she's been old enough to play, sitting at her mother's feet while she works, Léo has treasured things that fall to the floor. This jealously guarded plunder is kept in a little drawstring bag that Sidonie gave her. Jeanne isn't allowed to touch it. At the very most she can occasionally admire its contents, in respectful silence, when her daughter chooses to lay it out ceremoniously before her.

Apart from a few commonplace leaves muddled in with the other things but not of any real importance themselves, Léo's petals and feathers have distinctive characters and their own names, some of them quite unrelated to their appearance or their true identity. Carnation, Big Green, Mimi Toto, Duck, Big 'sturtium and Little 'sturtium,

Mimosa and Radish are her favourites and subject to her tender care. As she does with her doll, the child maintains passionate relationships with them, and has never-ending conversations that Jeanne doesn't understand at all but which seem to fascinate Toussaint now that he's at leisure to witness them. In the early days, Léo was intimidated and then irritated by her father's insistent stare, but she doesn't pay it the least attention now. She plays as she used to, relaxed and full of chat.

This Thursday, even though she insists she doesn't have colic, the child keeps interrupting her games to ask for the chamber pot. In the end, towards the middle of the afternoon, Toussaint hauls himself out of the armchair and beckons her.

Standing with the key in his hand, he wordlessly offers to take his daughter to the half landing one floor down. The smelly cubicle is shared by a dozen tenants in the building and Léo usually baulks at going there. The place disgusts and frightens her. But now, caught off guard and swayed by a combination of curiosity and eagerness to stave off boredom, she abandons her petals and allows herself to be led along the landing.

The door stays ajar and Jeanne, who's been at her flowers since dawn, stops to listen as the heavy footsteps and hesitant little feet head off down the dark stairwell. Léo's piping voice has reverted to its usual monologue, giving a running commentary on her progress, and it soon grows quieter with each stair she descends.

Jeanne finds herself home alone for a few minutes, and she hasn't been alone for nearly ten days. This fleeting solitude, this true silence which isn't just the absence of sound, these are things she has missed without realizing it.

She puts the ball down onto the heating pad and stretches her fingers and shoulders.

Toussaint has left the room at last. She wonders whether he'll make up his mind to face the outside world one day, whether he'll contemplate looking for work.

She's heard talk about badly injured men. Equipped with brand-new metal prosthetics, they've gone back to work in the fields. Some have no hands or arms, but can apparently handle tools, drink from a glass and carefully pick up their pipes. The poor men who've had a leg amputated can walk and even work the land. Someone's gone as far as inventing a foot shaped like a spade for their sake.

Toussaint certainly isn't that bad. He still has his hands, arms, legs and backbone. He can do everything. If he turned up at the shoe factory on rue Pixérécourt, Jeanne's sure they'd take him back. Despite his problems with speaking. Despite his mask.

She ought to tell him one of these days – that they won't make it on just her salary.

Now that the end of the war is in sight, you can bet the moratorium on rents won't last much longer. Coal, food, clothes – it's all so difficult to get hold of. Bread, milk, sugar and coal are rationed. Butchers have been closed for three days a week since May. Patisseries have disappeared. She's not sure her husband realizes. Paris is short of everything. Men on the streets hunt down discarded old crates to peel the metal strips from them. And old crates are rare, because people hang on to them or someone picks them up straight away and reduces them to puny bundles of firewood to burn in their own stoves or to sell.

With cold weather on the way, people salvage rabbit skins, they make tight balls of old paper for burning and even ransack trees. Jeanne, Sidonie and Léo went to strip bark from the plane trees along the edge of the Bois de Boulogne several times during the last few winters. Her mother has sent her the pelt of a poached fox from the farm in Replonges. Its red fur has a strong smell, but Jeanne has put it on her chair, where it keeps her backside warm.

Circumstances on the home front may bear no comparison with what soldiers experience on the front lines, but they've deteriorated with each passing year. Toussaint, whether in the trenches or in hospital, knew nothing of the life they led.

The war is nearly over, everything will go back to normal. Prices are bound to settle down, there'll be food again, perhaps they'll be given an allowance. But how can anyone be sure, and who knows if they'll last till then?

At about five in the evening Jeanne gets ready to make her delivery. She'll take Léo; she doesn't leave her by herself on Thursdays, even now that Toussaint's back.

On her way out she trips on the landing. There's a bundle wrapped in familiar striped fabric on the floor. It's Sidonie's aprons, bound up in a worn square of her-ringbone tweed. The parcel is usually plumper – this after-noon's must have barely a dozen and a half items in it.

Jeanne is thrown. The seamstress has never dumped her work without saying a word before. She usually comes in, chats, and dispenses endless advice to pass on to old Madame Aymard, the woman who oversees all the finished pieces that come in from homeworkers. And if Jeanne isn't at home, then Sidonie waits and comes back an hour or two later. That's their arrangement. To save on work time they take it in turns to make both their deliveries, because deliveries gobble up hours, and the best hours at that, when there's full daylight, when, if you stay at home at your table, you don't need to use up your lamp oil to get on with your orders. The time lost in deliveries and waiting at the workshop, the department store or with the contractor is always subtracted from sleep.

On this occasion the bundle has been left on the floor, like a corpse that Jeanne is in no hurry to recognize.

She goes to knock on Sidonie's door, but there's no reply. The whole framework of silence is infiltrated by the shrieks of two women quarrelling a few floors below. Léo, who's eager to get going, excited at the prospect of taking the Métro, bumps down the stairs on her bottom. She's already on the third floor. So Jeanne loses patience and walks away.

Her arms laden, she ploughs through the claggy smell of onions and fried herring that seems to have hung in the common parts of this building for ever, and heads off after her daughter on the slippery stairs.

The Métro's teeming with tired, hurrying people. There are no seats left in the second-class carriage that they've stepped into and as Jeanne lurches, encumbered by her parcels, she does her best to hold the child to her.

There's a young man of about twenty sitting on one of the central banquettes. The right-hand sleeve of his coat hangs limp, empty of flesh, and Jeanne, who's just made eye contact with him, automatically pictures the stump. She imagines that it may not be fully scarred yet and wonders if she'd have the courage to touch it.

Whether they're strolling in little clusters freshly discharged from hospital, hawking patriotic trinkets or hugging the walls as they hobble on their crutches, there are many war-wounded on the streets these days. Some are even reduced to begging on pavements.

Losing an arm is a tragedy for any human being, but much worse for a factory worker, Jeanne thinks, pinching her lips. From the look of the man on the seat, with his suggestion of a five o'clock shadow and his well-trimmed moustache, his faraway expression and his impeccably clipped nails – those he has left – she imagines he must be from a middle-class family, a student. The boy won't have trouble finding work in an office.

The doors open. Streams of passengers disperse onto the platform and others step inside. It's easier to breathe in the carriage now. Jeanne wedges her parcels into a more comfortable position and, because Léo has just buried her face in her skirts, strokes the child's head with the tips of her fingers. A dazed silence has settled around them, but it's soon bristling with stunned gesticulations and exclamations that Jeanne, lost in her thoughts, doesn't try to understand.

Next to her, though, a bulky woman with chubby cheeks looks poleaxed.

My poor friend, the woman exclaims all of a sudden.

My poor friend, you must be in so much pain.

Jeanne turns round. And he's there.

It's the first time she's seen one. A soldier of this particular breed. With no mask, no barriers.

With terrible facial injuries.

Incredible though it may seem, here the man is, in among the crowd, in all the raw horror of his injury. His face naked.

Eyes flit all around him, heads turn and flinch away, a half-pitying, half-appalled murmuring proliferates, swelling into an electrifying buzz.

And yet the wounded man stands tall, facing the window with unfocused eyes, avoiding his own reflection and those of other passengers.

The whole structure of his face has been destroyed. His nose with its widened base butts up against a staring eye that slumps onto his cheek. His mouth is drawn inwards and looks as if it's still reverberating from an almighty walloping. His chin is swollen with crinkles in a sinister waxy colour.

My poor friend, the fat woman keeps saying idiotically. Her voice rings out through the carriage, smothering the thrum of the engine. My *poor* friend.

And she goes up to the soldier, solemnly pats his shoulder.

Jeanne is filled with horror, far more from the woman's performance than the sight of this shapeless face.

While Léo presses herself still harder against her thigh, Jeanne can feel the man's tension expanding inside her own flesh and she drops a box of flowers, which falls to her feet without a sound.

It's as if the other woman is touching Jeanne herself.

She wishes she could scream, but not a sound, not a word comes to her. She wishes she'd never seen any of this, not the soldier, not the woman with her patting hand and horrified voice, not the faces looming around her, intact faces whose saddened smiles look like monstrous grimaces.

In this fog, a woman near her leans down to put herself on a level with the two young boys travelling with her. They haven't seen anything, these innocent creatures, so she tips them off with a tilt of her chin towards the soldier. To make sure they see. Sure they don't miss a thing. Sure the disabled man's agonizing bad luck edifies their future patriots' souls.

The Métro brakes and slows. The doors open and the injured man launches himself outside as if throwing himself into an abyss to escape it all. And when the train sets off again, everyone notices that the young man whose arm has been amputated has also left his seat.

The relief is palpable around Jeanne and Léo. People exchange conspiratorial looks and words.

You see plenty of war-wounded and disabled, dozens of them. But, it has to be said, he was really something. Oh yes. And no prosthesis. No false cheek or false nose, no false moustache to cover up. No glass eye. No scarf or bandaging.

As Léo relaxes her grip and crouches to pick up her mother's box of ranunculuses, the fat woman raises her voice and talks to her. And from the first words, everyone can tell she's addressing the whole carriage.

Did you see him, that poor soldier, did you see his hideous face, well, if our brave men are falling at all hours of day and night and bleeding and dying in the mud, well then, my girl, it's for *your* sake – at this point the woman gets more passionate, pointing at Léo and then turning towards the two little boys and their mother – and for *your* sakes too, my boys. Our soldiers are suffering so that you don't have to go through that suffering. That's right! It's to save our children that uncles and daddies are dying. Think about it, think about it long and hard. It's for your sakes.

16

When Jeanne and Léo get back to rue de la Lune on that first Thursday in November 1918, they're freezing, disorientated and soaked by the rain that started as soon as they emerged from the Métro station. Jeanne is so relieved to be home at last that it's several seconds before she notices the change.

She closes the door, puts her packages on the sideboard, sighs and gives herself a shake. The room is steeped in darkness and there's nothing surprising about that. Toussaint spends most of his time asleep or pretending to be, and he knows it's best to save on lamp oil.

But it's different this time, different shadows, a different silence.

Toussaint has evaporated.

Léo can rummage through the storeroom as much as she likes, and look behind, in and under the bed, but the man with the mask is invisible. So are his big military coat and his hat. She eyes her mother, who's busy adjusting the lamp, then goes and stands before the photo on the wall. Her hair drips cold droplets onto the shoulders of her cape.

There he is. Her real father, the one she's lived with for so long, the one she tells stories to in the same way that she treats her favourite petals to her endless litany of babbling. This soldier who fits perfectly under her child's hand when she lays it over him, disappearing and reappearing as the fancy takes her. That father.

And the one on the wall is always faithful – just as silent as the one with the mask, but his company is infinitely sweeter.

The stove is barely warm and the temperature in the room has plummeted. There isn't quite enough coal left to revive the fire and Jeanne doesn't have the heart for it either. So she quickly rubs her daughter's hair dry with an old towel, takes off her damp clothes and slips her under the eiderdown. The rust-coloured fox fur will have to stand in for a heater.

Léo lies shivering in bed, her eyes pinned on the photograph, and announces, He's gone.

He's gone, the other daddy has.

Jeanne doesn't know what to say or what to think. She feels hurt. Toussaint's unexpected absence, complicated by the sight of the man in the Métro, and amplified by the cold and dark that greeted them as they came into the room, has filled her with an obscure feeling of betrayal. For the ten days that he's sat here inert and unsettling, she's so longed for him to go out and bravely face up to the world. She's wanted that with all her might. So desperately that she's sometimes felt a crackle of anger run up and down her arms. She's had to restrain herself from shaking him and bundling him outside.

She also knows, or at least does her best to imagine, how much he suffered back there. In the war and in hospital. It's probably unfair to resent him now, but she can't repress an intense, ill-defined rancour rising from her navel to the back of her throat.

Why did he need to go out in secret? Behind her back? To run away in the rain, leaving the room infiltrated by these enemies, the cold and dark?

She looks on the table for a message, a folded piece of paper, the corner of a newspaper on which he might have written a note, a ready answer, kept in a pocket or curled in a fist for days.

A word to say where he's gone and when he plans to be back.

Just to say whether he plans to come back to her some day. Given that he lives here now. Given that he's healed, mended.

Jeanne looks for a note that would show consideration for her.

But the worktable, now cleared of the ranunculuses and waiting for the next batch of materials to be assembled, has nothing to say. Shaping balls, pliers, the bran-filled cushion, rubber pad, India rubber, silk thread and cotton thread wait obediently in her wooden workbox, next to the cold heater.

All she finds in the storeroom is her husband's kitbag and some of his clothes, hanging on hooks, ice cold.

Toussaint hasn't written a message.

*

She yanks off a hunk from the loaf of cheap bread she brought home. There's a bit of pâté left. A not very appealing carrot. That'll do for their supper.

The inside of her nose tickles maddeningly; she juts out her lower jaw, gliding the tip of her tongue over the base of her teeth. She's furious, almost crying, and all the more furious for almost crying. Crying for him. From being without him.

Toussaint. Toussaint. As if the name has changed. As if it's lying.

With a chipped plate in her hand, she slips into bed next to Léo and, although not able to appreciate it fully, rediscovers the child's warmth. Léo meanwhile immediately huddles up to her as if nothing has changed. It feels startlingly right for them to be united again, nestled together, and Jeanne remembers when Toussaint came home and she picked up her daughter and introduced her to her flesh-and-blood father. She felt more solid, more whole, more *Jeanne* if truth be told, with Léo in her arms.

She's not so sure this evening. Who she is. What's missing. Where her body is supposed to begin and end.

They lie in bed, slowly eating small mouthfuls of bread, some of them smeared with subtly rancid pâté. To her daughter's anxious surprise, Jeanne doesn't pay any attention to the crumbs that fall on the sheet.

So, to distract her, Léo wiggles the limp carrot comically, transforming it into a doll with a nasal voice and a single upright hair. When she eventually falls asleep, hugging her rag doll, the carrot top and the fox fur flecked with crumbs, Jeanne hauls herself out from the warmth of the bed.

Her loosened hair hangs to the middle of her back. Wearing nothing but a long shirt, a cardigan and woollen stockings, she goes out and trots furtively to Sidonie's door. She needs to give her the parcel from old Madame Aymard, eight dozen aprons ready to be stitched together. And ask how she is. And just see how she looks.

The temperature on the landing is bitter.

A hint of light filters under the door along with a fug of muffled sounds, voices, a laugh and peculiar singing. Jeanne knocks gently, using their usual code, three sharp raps then one more; but nothing happens other than a slow dwindling of the sound, and even on the third attempt Sidonie doesn't deign to stop what she's doing, still less to come to the door.

In the end, the parcel wrapped in fabric is left on the doorstep with a sigh.

Mother Birot opposite seems to be in. There's a strip of light under her door too.

But despite her urge to talk to someone about the state she's in, Jeanne runs home to throw herself into the bed.

It's a short night.

In the early hours of the morning, a few minutes before the alarm clock rings, Jeanne opens her eyes. A mass of sharpened crumbs prickles her shoulder. She feels heavy. She's never understood why dawn almost always finds her even more weary than when she went to bed. As if sleep and the quiet hours glide over her, restoring nothing. She stretches – her back is a hundred years old. Léo, lying in the crook of her arm, moves her head.

A smell of smoke, of burnt toast. The poker rummaging inside the stove. Without seeing it, Jeanne imagines the coal dust, anticipates the first wave of warmth when the stove has just been lit, the luminous glow that doesn't yet give off real heat but just flickers.

He's here.

He's brought things with him. Fatty things. Toasted things. Wet things. Bottles that shudder if he walks too close to where they stand against the wall on the tiled floor.

She closes her eyes again and knows that, only a moment earlier, Léo closed hers again too.

17

It's three o'clock in the afternoon and Toussaint, wearing his old leather shoes, his military coat and a canvas hat, has just gone out onto the landing and closed the door.

He goes down the stairs. He's leaving. He's leaving again.

As he went out, he nodded to Jeanne, who's sitting at a new poppy construction site. It was a quick tilt of his head accompanied – although, in hindsight, Jeanne can't be sure of this – by a soft grunt.

There's still a white mask hiding his face, but when Jeanne looked up at him, she noticed that he'd discreetly changed it. The one he's wearing now is spotless. When she woke this morning she saw that he'd stained the old one. Right there, at the corner of his mouth. With soot and wine. Or perhaps blood.

Wherever it was he went the day before, Toussaint had tracked down a bushel of coal, some milk, two litres of cider and some charcuterie. He'd relit the stove and fried thin rashers of bacon in the pan.

Maybe it was to soften her up, but even though she felt overwhelmingly hungry when the fatty smell permeated the room, Jeanne did her best to keep her appetite a secret. All she offered was a sulky pout. Some ostentatious yawning. And endless kisses in the crook of Léo's neck and her dishevelled hair to hide her face, so that she didn't have to look at him as he stood by the stove turning over thick slices of bread and prodding the bacon with the end of a fork.

Later, as she walked home from Léo's nursery school on her own, she slowed down despite the wet weather. She was afraid to go home. Afraid of opening the door onto a deserted room. Afraid also that he'd still be there with his bacon and his burnt bread. Irritated by the fact that she still didn't know how to react, that she'd allowed herself to be swept up in this habit of silence. Toussaint is forcing her not to talk either.

In the end, though, she climbed up the four flights of stairs.

And there he was. Lying in the middle of the bed, asleep, with the no longer perfectly white mask pushed to one side – but not far enough to show a suggestion of his hidden skin, even when she looked more closely. He was snoring, but not as he used to. The air in his sinuses was obstructed, churning its way out.

She stood and nibbled at the bacon and bread, watching him out of the corner of her eye. His coat was still wet, lying on the floor near the sideboard. She kicked it aside angrily as she passed it.

And now he's just gone out.

He's no longer hiding from her, but doesn't say where he's going.

He's gone.

Jeanne pins up a plait that's come loose, straightens a hair comb, then dresses quickly, wrapping a scarf tightly around her neck. She tiptoes downstairs.

Once outside she sets off in pursuit of him, concentrating on adopting the right pace, maintaining the appropriate distance. She must keep Toussaint in her sights without being spotted.

Before the war she often found herself tailing him, always in this same strange way, launching after him, irresistibly. And not only on that morning just after Bella died when, stunned and devastated, she watched him collapse against a wall in tears. There were so many other times.

She just liked watching him without his knowing. Never tired of watching him.

When Toussaint was off somewhere, he never dreamed that she might be there on that street corner, behind those arches, that she secretly devoured him with her eyes, revelling in the shape of him from a distance. He was another man then, another man in another body, his voice, his stride, the very texture of him unfamiliar. Jeanne felt just as much desire for her husband as for this other Toussaint who moved about, a whole new person and free of her weight.

As if from the very start there had been two completely distinct Toussaints and both were objects of her desire.

*

She follows him along rue Beauregard, then he turns right towards boulevard Poissonnière, and so does she. And it's as she is following twenty paces behind him that she has a true measure of all the time that has passed, all the events each of them has experienced, in his or her own way. Because this Toussaint in front of her is no longer the old Toussaint.

She knew that, of course she knew it, after so many silent impenetrable days, but she couldn't help naively imagining that outside, without her, he'd revert to the man he was in July 1914, striding gamely across Paris, greeting an acquaintance every now and then, his eyes bright and his face open. And as she sneaks along behind him she's suddenly struck by the expression she happened to alight on. His face open.

Toussaint walks along the pavement with his head lowered and his back slightly bent. He's turned up his collar. He treads slowly.

She thought it every time: before, whenever he walked, it was really him walking. There he was, impatient and blindingly alive. And now he's lost his distinctive stride, he moves cautiously, putting one foot in front of the other as if something's broken, perhaps the balls of his feet, perhaps his whole skeleton and the flesh anchored to it. Or perhaps, and this is a strange thought for her to have, as if he needs to be careful with the very fabric of the pavement, more fragile than skin.

Jeanne hasn't seen him move for such a long time. At home he walks only three paces, has no momentum and never goes anywhere. He's always too close by.

His shoulders. She doesn't recognize his shoulders either. How could she have thought he'd grown, the evening he came home? It's the opposite, he's shrunk.

Either way, she keeps following him.

And all at once the thing she's been dreading without admitting it to herself happens.

On the corner of rue Saint-Fiacre there is a cluster of people waiting to cross the street. Still hanging back, Jeanne doesn't pay them much attention until Toussaint's walk becomes a lurch. On this tip-off she looks up and widens her field of vision. The people are calling out to her husband. With the racket they're making, other passers-by turn to look, their eyes converging on the group and then coming to rest on the spotless white of Toussaint's mask.

The scene in the Métro plays out again just as it must play out a hundred times a day for every man with this sort of injury who ventures out. But neither Jeanne nor Toussaint is prepared for it.

After a moment of jigging on the spot like a panicking horse, Toussaint quickens his pace and flees. Jeanne goes after him, and catches a few words as she passes the gawkers.

The courage. That man. Good God, the courage.

And she can tell that if she slows down, apparently open to what they're saying, offering an obliging ear, they'd call her as a witness without knowing. They'd resuscitate the mayor's high-blown words, probe the wounds, pick off the scabs. Stir the blood. She'd be spattered with it right up to her face and down her neck. She'd have no air left to breathe, no shelter to slink to in peace.

She'd be burned too. Indirectly.

She hurries on, clutching her fists to her chest, almost running. Her shoes pinch her ankles painfully.

Opening up an inky tunnel, Toussaint's dark silhouette draws away ahead of her.

What do they want from him? What have they done to him?

She wants to catch up with him now, to throw herself at his back, put her arms around him, bury her mouth and teeth in the wool of his coat, thud her jawbone against his ribcage, she wants to stop him, to take him, they'd throw themselves against a wall, right here, the two of them, bowled over, far away from other people. She thinks that in this embrace, in this sudden annihilation, they would finally rediscover each other.

She's running now. She feels she might fall over right in the middle of the boulevard, her muscles are so tense she's about to collapse. Toussaint's going to turn round and find her there, rolled onto her back, burst open like a piece of plump overripe fruit, her legs splayed under her heavy skirt, drawing everyone's attention to herself, to herself and then to him.

But Toussaint's just vanished.

Jeanne had glanced over at the trams forming a dark moving bulk in the far lane as they drew closer, and now she's gone and lost him. Without him, the boulevard is deserted. She reels on the pavement for a moment, her eyes like a drunk's, a taste of decay in her mouth.

There he is, though, she can see him through the cafe window, at the back, standing with his feet in the sawdust. He's toppled into the world of All men.

He has his back to Jeanne and she stands there, breathless, studying him through the railings daubed with black paint, through the window speckled from recent rain and through the smoke that fills the room packed with people. He's not alone. There are two men with him; they smile at the sight of him and nod energetically.

She notices, homing in on him from every direction, the insistent stares to which she's now so sensitive. But when she looks closely at the two strangers, who, to her surprise, have casually put a hand on each of the new arrival's shoulders, she guesses where they know each other from and why they arranged to meet up in this cafe on boulevard Poissonnière, just beyond the Parisiana.

They look more or less the same age, although it's difficult to tell from their faces. They're glad to see each other. They're blood brothers. They're all disfigured.

Jeanne can't tell from behind whether Toussaint is actually talking to them, but his shoulders twitch and his arms gesticulate in the yellow light, perhaps – who knows – complementing a flood of words too long withheld. The sight of those two men, cleaved open by grimaces, teeth and blinking eyes, constricts Jeanne's throat.

And when the more damaged of the two suddenly catches her eye in the distance, she looks away as if she's been slapped.

Toussaint's going to turn round and see her, she's sure he is. He'll think she's spying on him and, for the first time, it won't be very far from the truth.

But on the other side of the window, at the back of the bar, she's already been forgotten. The conversation has picked up again. The poor man must have to put up with that sort of thing so often, stares like hers with their combination of horror and fascination. When all's said and done, the way Jeanne was looking isn't all that different from anyone else.

The three men sit themselves at a table, and in the never-ending parcel of time that Jeanne spends planning to walk away but not actually succeeding in doing so, they chat, play dominoes and knock back small glasses of spirits.

In the end she crosses the boulevard to take up a sheltered position opposite. While she gradually succumbs to the clutches of the cold, she starts to feel uncomfortable. She can't remember why she came here, and doesn't know how to interpret what she appears to have found. And it isn't another woman igniting this jealousy – a jealousy that's got her right here, in her stomach – but two disfigured soldiers, two poor bastards almost too painful to look at.

Night is closing in.

Jeanne paces up and down on the pavement. Remembering old man Caillet's description, she makes a real effort to picture the day room where these three soldiers lived side by side for months, perhaps for the entire time that Toussaint spent there, at Val-de-Grâce. What they went through together – the pain, the hope, the exhaustion and the terror – will never be hers, will never be accessible to her. And it's only now that Jeanne realizes this.

However convincingly she imagines a succession of metal-framed beds populated by bloodied, bandaged faces, the white figures of nurses and the goatee beard of a portly, overworked surgeon, she knows she's a lifetime away from the real thing. Even if Toussaint suddenly started talking, spent day and night describing what happened, in the trenches as well as in hospital, what he saw, what was done to him and how he lived, this space would still be beyond her reach. A whole chunk of this man's life is destined to stay dark. Absolutely impenetrable.

She puts her hands over her face and through her fingers inhales the cold, damp smell of Paris mingled with her own smell. She wonders whether all soldiers' wives have come to this – sniffing their skin while waiting for a husband who's been replaced by a stranger. Whether her situation is unusual, worse than other people's. Or whether she should count herself lucky that he's back, her Toussaint, even with an invisible face.

What those men went through together, what they're still experiencing now, and the future that's mapping itself out for them – it all leaves the rest of the world by the wayside.

But they used to be just one body, the two of them, and now she's ended up outside. Jeanne and Toussaint. Toussaint and Jeanne.

There were three of them. Toussaint, Jeanne and Bella. Toussaint, Jeanne and Léonie.

Now the injury fills every scrap of space.

18

Word is the Spanish flu will end up culling the young.

Word is French chemists have found terrifying ways to polish off the Boche.

Word is people are growing beans and carrots on place du Panthéon.

Word is bread is so acid that it sours whatever you dunk it in.

Word is, now they've got their English-style working week, the next thing the workers'll want is an eight-hour day.

Word is the munitionettes earned a fortune in their factories.

Word is if this goes on much longer, a kilo of steak will be more than seven francs.

Word is it'll never stop raining.

Word is they threw sweets stuffed with typhus and cholera from their aeroplanes.

Word is no one'll ever have enough hate in their hearts for them.

Word is plenty of women found comfort in other men's arms when their soldier husbands were away.

Word is there'll soon be no potatoes left.

19

Jeanne gives up in the end. From where she stands on the pavement opposite, her eyes relinquish the halo of light spilling from the Parisiana and the distant yellow rectangle where Toussaint seems to be coming back to another life.

She walks away from the boulevard and goes to pick up Léo.

The child's waiting for her on a bench in the covered yard at her nursery school, her back slumped, her beret askew and with a length of hair ribbon that's come undone trailing over one shoulder. She watches Jeanne cross the playground but doesn't run over to her or even get up. She sits surly-faced, swinging her legs under a dress that's too long for her. She's the last child in the grey, deserted playground. Her mother's late for the second time this week.

Fat widow Masson, who's responsible for greeting the children and releasing them at the end of the day, is sweeping the playground half-heartedly, but drops her shovel and broom as soon as she sees Jeanne. Before Jeanne even reaches her, she assails her with criticism, turning into a snarling animal with rolling eyes.

But Jeanne is in no mood for it. Engulfed by a dense fog, she's in no mood for anything. The widow's shouts roll over her like water. And when the final assault is a scruffily tied-up parcel wrapped in newspaper thrown at her chest, she hardly even blinks. She gives a suggestion of what's intended to be a humble smile, nods, takes her daughter by the hand and scuttles away without a word.

Léo's soiled herself again.

They walk home through the darkened streets. Léo – who's starving, whiny and not properly cleaned up – trots along behind her mother, who restrains her urge to drop the foul-smelling package in the gutter.

Jeanne feels so tired, being back here in Belleville. Before the war, she often used to walk past the nursery schools in this neighbourhood. She'd be pushing Bella or a baby Léo in a pram or carrying them on one hip, and she'd stop and gaze enviously at the mothers surrounded by their little ones, like queen bees. Some would buy a handful of mint pastilles or chocolates at the refreshment stall and share them with their children, eating them right there on the pavement. And watching them, Jeanne anticipated the pleasure of adopting these same rituals as soon as her daughter was old enough.

She could see herself in the street, sucking on boiled sweets with Bella. She'd be holding her hand.

Léo would have been given a gold star.

Bella would have pretty curls framing a solemn face.

Léo would twitter away, telling her all the little things that had happened at school.

Bella would be wearing a new pinafore in black cotton satin.

But nothing happened as it should have. Bella didn't get the chance to go to nursery school, and Léo, now in her second year, doesn't like her teacher at all. What she says about her is neither kind nor amusing. It's actually slightly worrying. And Jeanne doesn't always have the energy to come up with calming or reassuring arguments. Sometimes she doesn't even know how to cope with it. She wishes she could block her ears.

As for sweets, what with the shortage of sugar and the rise in prices, they've been beyond her means for a long time.

School. Jeanne's just about glad to know that Léo gets a free meal at lunchtime.

She feels swindled. It was all lies. She didn't understand. Neither she nor her daughters have managed to make the most of it.

With her shoulders hunched to protect herself from the cold and everything else, she remembers what she thought she knew about life, before the war. Not that life was ever easy, but Jeanne wishes she could stop thinking about how, back then, Sidonie still had a son. That back then Toussaint talked all the time and held her in his arms.

Before the war. After the war. She's had enough of talking about and thinking about the before and after. They're sapping all the life force from her.

*

When mother and daughter reach the fourth floor and open the door, Toussaint isn't yet home. Neither of them is surprised.

Jeanne lights the lamp. The room's a mess, the chamber pot is overflowing, there's a smock waiting to be patched on the back of the armchair and the tiles around the stove are darkened by a dusting of burnt toast crumbs. Two dozen milky-pink poppies are still drying on a line across one corner of the room, while the rest of them, the unfinished ones, are piled up around the heater.

She sighs. She's lost another couple of hours' work.

She'll have to go and fetch water and improvise a rudimentary bread soup.

She'll have to clean up the child and wash the soiled dress, so that in the morning she can return the one that's been lent to Léo and which hangs pitifully from her meagre frame.

She'll have to sit up till dawn making poppies.

Clutching her pitcher, Jeanne starts by heading out onto the landing and knocking at Sidonie's door. As she predicted, her neighbour doesn't answer. Impatient, she immediately heads off and noisily descends two of the flights of stairs she's just struggled up and exchanges a passing word with another tenant. The woman's got wind of the story – she knows about the mutilated face and suddenly assails Jeanne's retreating back with some words that will be difficult to forget.

Jeanne grits her teeth, closes her eyes and forges on towards the water pump through a stench of boiled cabbage.

The finest, most beautiful love is the love we build on pity. There, that's what other people are saying, what they're thinking, perhaps. She'll never manage it.

She didn't know she was going to do this. She thought she was just tired.

Léo's standing by the unmade bed, watching, blinking repeatedly. The woman's eyelashes are separated out into shiny spikes. Her dark eyes – wide open one minute and veiled the next – are circled by coppery pools. There's a pinkish trickle coming from one of her nostrils. Her face is swollen. And the imprisoned air is released from her lungs in short, loud bursts.

The world has just turned upside down.

When her mother gets back with the pitcher full of ice-cold water, Léo's already on all fours on the floor, mumbling quietly, with her whole collection of petals and feathers spread out around her.

Jeanne closes the door, pours water in the basin, adjusts the lamp, then collapses in the armchair and unlaces her too-tight shoes. It's only when she looks up that she notices.

Half of the poppies hanging to dry head-down from a line above the table have disappeared.

Jeanne jumps up and immediately flies into a whirl of fury. She doesn't mean to, doesn't think about it, but seems to explode into a thousand rabid particles. She sweeps Léo up off the floor. The slap flies, followed by one, two, three more. She loses count. She's not counting anything. Nothing counts.

They're both shredded by her anger.

The child isn't allowed to touch anything on the table, and especially not finished flowers, whether they're hanging to dry or already lying in their boxes. She must respect her mother's work. She knows that.

Jeanne roars.

She can't take any more of this life. For months now she's felt as if she's being dragged down into the depths. Léo's a dirty little girl, a horrible baby and a thief who's ruining her life, can't she see her mother's working herself to the bone day and night, her father doesn't even have a face anymore, and the whole country's suffering while she's messing around stealing poppies? Can't she see anything? And she stinks too, at her age! She's ugly and hideous and smells bloody disgusting and Jeanne can't take anymore.

But however persistent she is, however much she threatens and then begs and bawls, the child just cowers. She doesn't say anything about the flowers, about what she did with them and where she can possibly have put them.

And Léo is now indistinguishable from the silent Toussaint.

The shouting has stopped. Jeanne has thrown herself across the bed, surrendering her convulsive rage to the eiderdown. Sitting on the threshold of the storeroom as if she's fallen there, Léo just stays still, not looking at her mother. Not looking at anything. Every now and then her tongue sneaks out, up to her nose, which is still seeping mucus. Her chequered pinafore and her dress are wet and cold. At her feet a big puddle is forming from the water Jeanne hurled over her.

It's like the aftermath of a battle that they've both lost.

Later, try as she might to think things through calmly, to check everything over, to count and recount the flowers in their boxes and on the order form, Jeanne just can't find them. And yet she's missing nine pink poppies as wide as her hand and as soft as a kiss.

20

At first light, when Jeanne's about to go downstairs for the milk, Mother Birot pops out onto the landing. Anyone would think she was spying on her.

The old woman's worried. It's three days, she says, since Sidonie's given any sign of life, except for a bundle of aprons left outside a door. That's not normal. She's not using the communal latrine or emptying her chamber pot. She's stopped going out for provisions. The caretaker downstairs has confirmed that she hasn't been past her lodge. It's as if she's evaporated into thin air.

Even so, there's no doubt about it. Sidonie's there. Mother Birot says that, down her end of the corridor, she can hear her talking through the walls.

Yes, talking. Goodness knows who to, but she talks.

If Jeanne came closer she'd hear her too.

Huddled together, they press themselves up to the seamstress's door, straining their ears. Wedged under Jeanne's inquisitive chin is the old woman's fibrous shoulder, along with its sour smell as dense as flesh.

They listen.

But there's no light filtering through the glass pane, no

thrum of the sewing machine or household activity coming through the wood panels.

It's still very early. Sidonie must be asleep, Jeanne protests, chewing her lip. She feels guilty.

What if her friend is slumped on her chair like a stunned animal? What if she has nothing left to eat? Or she's dead? What if, just for a change, she's gone down with Spanish flu on top of her grief?

Sidonie. Since going to the town hall and the subsequent tears, Jeanne's been carried away with her own upheavals and has completely neglected her.

Sidonie.

The previous evening, when Toussaint finally came home, Jeanne had already returned to her poppies. The sun and her fury had gone down long since.

Toussaint smelt of tobacco and the outside world. She didn't get close enough to determine what his mouth smelt like, but could guess he'd been knocking back strong wine. As he moved about the room, the one cheek of his that she could see shifted from red with alcohol and the cold back to its usual pallor.

He didn't look at her and she tried not to look at him. Not seeing him was difficult, because he drew her eye. But she didn't say anything and, thanks to a dogged persistence, managed to render him as good as invisible.

All she'd left for his supper was a slice of toast and the greasy edge of some pâté. He ate on his feet, sniffing, with his back to her. He came across as heavy, heavy with light and heavy from the street. When he sat on the side of the bed and unlaced his boots, Jeanne couldn't help scanning the rim of the sole for specks of sawdust from the cafe on boulevard Poissonnière. But they'd all gone.

The floor next to the table hadn't finished drying the great puddle of her anger. An exhausted Léo was asleep in her cot.

Jeanne looked away and went back to work on her petals.

The shaping ball was black and hot. Mirroring its rolling action with her chest and calibrating it with her breathing, she put the end of its handle between two ribs, under her breast. Every autumn and winter, during her busiest period, this part of her harboured a painful red patch from the endlessly repeated gesture as she bored powerfully into the bran-filled cushion until she achieved the perfect, delicate arch in the petals, two by two.

So some things came in pairs, and worked by adopting the same curve. Some things were soft and pink around a black heart.

Because they can't hear anything from the landing, Mother Birot coaxes Jeanne to her room and Jeanne slips into her home for the first time. The old woman is feral. No one sets foot on her territory. If she engages in conversation, it's in the courtyard, on the stairs or on her doorstep with the door barely open. No one ventures any further.

In February 1917 it was so bitterly cold that for two weeks the four of them slept together – Jeanne, Léo, Sidonie and the old woman spooning against each other in the seamstress's only bed, in an acrid stench that the cold didn't succeed in silencing, even though it could trundle ice along the Seine. And on these occasions, as she always did, Mother Birot accepted her neighbour's hospitality without reciprocating by inviting any of them to drink so much as a glass of milk in her home.

But today, if she wants Jeanne to hear what's going on through the walls, she'll just have to allow an invasion of her home. To reveal her paltry bed covered in lace, the cherished portrait of her father and – sprawling all around the stove and clumsily disguised under squares of canvas – her piles of onions and firewood, spilling about them their red skins on the one hand and scrawny twigs still green with sap on the other.

In all likelihood, Sidonie has withdrawn into the end room where her sons used to sleep, the one Jeanne has known only as Eugène's bedroom. This room has no common boundary with her own home, which explains why she hasn't heard the noises.

In fact, these last few days, she's had no idea what Sidonie's been doing.

In Mother Birot's room they press their cheeks to the wall covering, each at her own height. Their eyes are intense, open wide, immobilized by their need to understand. After a good minute, suddenly alighting deep inside their ears, the frizzy little sound of a voice makes its way through the thickness of bricks and tattered paper.

It's as if someone's singing on the other side. The tone is trembling, describing endless, vaguely familiar loops pitched somewhere between ecclesiastical dirges and Léo's droning when she twirls around the furniture with her doll.

Sidonie's voice, but different.

Mother Birot knocks on the wall but doesn't succeed in interrupting this great spool of song or even making it deviate by one iota. There seem to be words associated with the monotonous chant, they seem to flow like water from a fountain.

The old woman says it never stops, never stops, it's enough to drive her mad on her side of the wall, even at night when she wants to sleep. In the dark, this singing worms its way under the covers and comes to lick her face with its cold tongue. It's not so much that it's annoying her, not any more. It's starting to frighten her.

Jeanne gives three sharp raps on the mustard-and-gherkin wallpaper, and then one more – but nothing.

Four hours later, when the morning's heading towards afternoon, Jeanne finally hears Sidonie walk back into her front room.

Toussaint is asleep, lying full length on the bed, Léo's at school and Mother Birot is at the workroom. She and Sidonie are the only people awake on their floor.

She's out on the landing; she hasn't knocked and she hasn't called. She's pressed herself bodily against the door, not just her ear and her face but the flat of both hands, her breasts, her stomach and the curled tips of her toes. Blood is the first thing to penetrate the wood, its beating in her own body, and then, somewhere in front of her, echoing it, feet rocking on the sewing machine's treadle.

She's there, a few metres away, just behind the door.

She's stopped singing. She's just working, in silence. Sewing patiently.

Jeanne murmurs her name, with its long, weighty syllables; she scrapes the layers of yellow paint with her nails, three sharp scratches and then one more. She waits patiently. And all at once, drawing the chill air of the room in her wake, Sidonie comes to the door and lifts the latch.

It looks as if Sidonie's pleased to see her, because she's standing on tiptoe and smiling, her eyes on Jeanne's mouth.

But it's not true. Something about her face strikes a false note.

Jeanne feels awkward. She straightens her shawl over her chest, steps inside and closes the door, then glances around the room. The window is firmly closed, the stove door open, and under its twisted waves of white sheets the bed gapes like an animal's jaws. The fabric slung into all four corners has gone. But what there is now is something in the air, a sad smell, a sad colour that brings a lump to the throat.

Sidonie is in a nightdress. Her black hair has come loose in a mass that lolls over her shoulders; the skin on her arms gleams in the half-darkness, divided into reddish patches, as if she's scratched herself, and intensely white areas that might almost be covered in chalk powder. Her wide, grey feet stand naked on the red tiles.

With all her warmth and density, Jeanne draws Sidonie to her. She can feel the seamstress's slack belly and breasts, and the winter-cold of her flesh, as she whispers into her ear and neck, proffering the muddle of words that comes to her.

She says she's sorry. Says she's missed her. She's been thinking all sorts, Jeanne has, and her fear's been swelling and thumping inside her head, so loudly. And Sidonie mustn't ever, no, absolutely never, stay tucked away, behind her closed door, all hidden and lonely and sad with no fire, not eating, not drinking and not saying anything.

Sidonie accepts this with a simple nod of her head. Jeanne hugs her close and then, holding her at arm's length, looks at her. It's Eugène who's been flowing over her cheeks in a tide of misery. Eugène and all the others who've left her in the lurch, ravaging her good flesh when it's still fresh. Jeanne gently strokes her face with the tips of her warm fingers.

Then she sits Sidonie down, puts on her bed jacket, pulls the cover towards her and lays it over Sidonie's knees, slides her nimble fingers through her hair to untangle it and plaits it loosely. She thinks again and lifts the nightdress. On your feet, she says, one foot up, and she pulls on a pair of stockings that were lying on the floor, cardboard-hard with old sweat.

She needs to get some warmth into her. Some warmth and some bread.

*

The stove is reverting to its slow purr, and the water, growing tepid in the pan, is waiting to have something – whatever can be cobbled together from the old dresser or goodness knows where – plunged into it. Sidonie gets to her feet, and the woollen blanket tumbles to the foot of the armchair. Reaching out her hands as if being reunited with a loved one, she goes over to the sewing machine that she tore herself away from when Jeanne arrived. She flumps onto the chair and slaps her worn feet on the cast-iron treadle. A rectangle of blue and grey cotton is soon darting back and forth under the presser foot and the needle.

When Jeanne comes over with a long spoon in her hand, the first things that strike her are the uncharacteristic, ragged seams and the way the thread – plying one way, then the other – whirs into clusters of curls. Then she notices paper padding poking out from the fabric; she thinks she recognizes the edge of a ration card for charcoal or milk. Sidonie mutters into her pale chin and bats aside Jeanne's intrusively inquisitive hand.

Next Jeanne opens the door to the bedroom, the one at the end. She opens the door wide and takes a step back, turning to Sidonie to secure her unspoken permission to go in and look. Over at the far side of the room, quite unexpectedly, a candle is burning.

But the seamstress is still hunched over her work and the only reply she offers is her back struck through by a listless plait.

Jeanne goes in.

There are two beds, one with its thin, pissage-stained mattress left bare. The other still has its eiderdown, bolster and flounced cushion – all of them only very slightly faded. A man's peaked cap has been placed in the middle. Against the wall, to one side of the window with its half-drawn curtains, a washstand on narrow feet, topped with a lace mat, acts as a pedestal for the lighted candle thrust into a candlestick.

She takes a few steps. Daylight penetrates weakly through the murky windowpanes. The smell is of dust and soot.

It's a chapel of rest.

An altar.

And pinned onto the wallpaper, rising all the way to the ceiling, or simply arranged on the table, are the relics.

The photograph of Eugène as a soldier has pride of place in the middle, wreathed by a circle of older photos, full-grown men and boys with solemn faces. A carved shell casing engraved with thistles, a large black crucifix, drips of white wax everywhere, a whole copse of boxwood sprigs saved from successive Palm Sundays and tied with a ribbon, open fans, handwritten letters embroidered over in red thread, long garlands of fabric flowers and stars, and a glued-together statuette of the Virgin and Child. River pebbles. A horn-handled knife. A folded handkerchief. A dried butterfly. A pipe. A wooden rosary. A certificate of honour. A spinning top. And there, in a jug, nine pink silk poppies, lent a yellow glow by the light of the flickering flame.

Jeanne's eyes narrow and fill with tears.

Without a sound, walking on tiptoe, Sidonie has appeared behind her and she starts singing her mad-woman's song again, prancing about the room.

Her fingers are as stiff as a doll's. Her shrill voice flits and swoops. Her face is filled with light.

21

In the end Jeanne closed the door and went home. Under the blanket there's heavy breathing, and still the same outline, like a fallen tree.

She stands in the middle of the room and the familiar surroundings swirl before her eyes.

She can see and smell the still-warm stove; see the lifeless poppies, some of which are missing, on the table and the drying line, and the three earthenware jugs lined up on the sideboard, filled with artificial roses and some of the most beautiful flowers ever created by her own two hands. She sees the military coat on a hook, a bluish section of it poking out from the storeroom; the mirror, the bottles, the saucepan and frying pan, the photograph of a soldier hanging a metre above the floor, within Léo's reach; the cot, which stands empty, with the doll in the middle of it, its arms open wide.

Jeanne picks up the small sunken pillow. The child's cherished drawstring bag is hidden underneath it. She eases out the string and opens it, just a little. Looks inside. Petals and feathers. Carnation, Big Green, Mimi Toto, Duck, Big 'sturtium and Little 'sturtium, Mimosa and Radish. And the nameless green leaves at the bottom.

Her energy's drained away. She sits at her table and tries to get back to the rolling, assembling and crinkling, but her fingers can't make the movements work.

She sits herself down on the edge of the bed and breathes loudly in turn. Their two rhythms of breathing expand within the room, occasionally falling into step with each other. The clock says it's two in the afternoon.

She undresses.

In her undershirt, she climbs softly onto the bed and slips beneath the eiderdown. Toussaint is lying on his front, his face turned towards her. The mask covers the upper half. His ample man's shirt is corkscrewed around his bulk like a skin of withheld words.

Two o'clock.

One Sunday in the summer of 1913 they'd ended up lying side by side like this at this exact time of day. It was under a tree, she remembers in a flash. They'd set out with some other families to spend the day by the river near Nogent.

Toussaint fell asleep first, his face flushed with the heat, fresh air and drink, and half hidden by yellowed grass. His shirtsleeves were rolled up above his elbows, and the shadows of leaves flittered lazily over his back and his skin with its gleam of sweat. Somewhere over there, squealing quietly, children played, also dazed by the sun.

Jeanne had tipped backwards carefully, lying alongside Toussaint, on her back, looking up at the sky. The scorched smell of hay and earth wafted to her. She turned to face him and watched him sleep for a while. An ant wended its way over the unevenly scythed meadow of his cheek.

Bella had been dead sixty-three days.

That child with her tiny little life – Jeanne hadn't had time to secure an image of her on paper, but had only the memory, now mingled with her father's soft snores, of her strained breathing and the velvety softness of her neck.

As she watched the ant approach Toussaint's lips, which still glistened from their snack and the cider, she thought about her daughter.

She didn't cry.

For several weeks her body had been growing firm and hot, hummingly alive as a bud on a vine. But in spite of her taut breasts, her apparent tiredness and her lack of appetite, Toussaint hadn't noticed anything.

She took his hand with its blackened nails, opened it wide and rested it there, well below her breasts. In the moment when her eyes were about to close, Toussaint's opened, and they looked at each other. She just kept her lips sealed and that nigella-flower blue flooded over her. She fell asleep straight away.

Jeanne leans over Toussaint in bed.

Toussaint's sleep, something vast and pure.

If she wanted to, she could peel off the mask without his noticing. Along the edge, by the border of the fabric, the thwarted beginnings of a lip are outlined, then, gaping, afford glimpses of an undersea cavity. She could slip inside there. She could discover this scar at last, drink it in. If he doesn't want to offer it to her, well, she could take it from him.

She reaches out her hand, skims the hot, rough skin of his chin. Through the wall, the sewing machine keeps up its constant thrum, while the familiar refrain of the rag-and-bone man drifts through the window.

Toussaint doesn't move. He's fast asleep, buried so deep he might never resurface.

She's not afraid. Not of him or his injury.

In the early days, yes, she tried to imagine what it might look like under there. The mush of flesh and clotted blood, the contortion, the gaping skin – she might never have recovered from the sight of it.

And then her disgust and terror gradually slackened. Because nothing was more painful than Sidonie's phantom-child lament or more monstrous than this white mask.

But to take it in these circumstances, like a thief, no, she doesn't want to.

She calls his name.

She calls his name until he jolts awake and sits up. She didn't mean to terrify him, but that's what happens when she says his name for the fifth time, raising her voice: he quails like a hunted animal and blurts a bear-like grunt from his misshapen throat.

She doesn't try to reassure him. Eyes him calmly, swallowing hard and a little too quickly, but standing her ground. She waits for him to come round and when the scab of fear and sleep has fallen away from him, she closes her eyes and concentrates with all her might on his mouth as it was before, the one that was, for example, described in his military records book as 'full'.

It well and truly was. It was full of her, his mouth, and for all those years Jeanne was full of Toussaint's mouth.

She takes something from under the sheet, puts it over her face and knots it clumsily at the back of her head, in her hair. It's the first mask, the one that he stained with smoke and wine the other day. In a quiet moment she washed it carefully, rubbing it with black soap and water until the stains were gone, then she dried it out flat in the secrecy of her skirt, against the rounded flesh of her thigh.

She's put it on crooked. The mirror's too far away to set it straight. Toussaint is all the mirror she has.

She's used this strip of cloth to cover the width of her mouth, her left cheek and a good part of her nose. Her lips open under the fabric and make it move with a volley of invisible words.

Their eyes jink away when they collide, but gradually settle and find each other as the furious thudding of their hearts subsides. Jeanne leans towards him and he backs away, tensing. Each time she pulls back he sits up again. It's a sort of game in which nobody laughs. Their calibrated eye contact forms a taut thread between them, and they sway at either end of it. One wide strap of Jeanne's undershirt rises and slips aside, suggesting the curve of a white shoulder.

Toussaint is pitched headlong into Jeanne's irises, bouncing from one to the other. Nothing exists now but their two colours. The blue of wild chicory and the brown of stripped wood.

Under Jeanne's mask, her breathing has created a wide bandage of hot fug. She reaches one hand towards Toussaint, towards his cheek, the covered side, and a sort of sob mixed in with bubbles and bone swells deep inside him.

The pillow he's just lifted his head from has made half his hair stand on end, and Jeanne smooths it down with small, gentle strokes, her fingers gathering the last mists of sleep as they leave. Toussaint hasn't moved, he hardly even quivers when she touches him.

But as her cupped hand moves downwards, gathering courage as it reaches the lip of fabric, Toussaint snatches her by the arm, his hand flying out in front of him as quick and beak-sharp as a bird of prey.

Jeanne's eyes immediately fill with a scalding film of water. She wishes she could stop him witnessing this performance, wishes her eyes were safely behind the mask with her mouth and nose and cheek; and she recoils, unsure how much of what she feels is shame and how much anger.

Through the far wall, Sidonie's humming, which had stopped, has started up again with new vigour.

Jeanne grits her teeth, groans with frustration and tears off her mask along with a plume of long brown hair. What a ridiculous idea that was. She resents him for that too, for her hope.

Then, her whole body tingling with a dark fire that flashes in her eyes, she arches towards his, talons out, chin tilted up.

But Toussaint stays stone-still, his hands resting one on top of the other over his chest, like sheets of paper. He's not looking at her. His pupils are locked onto the poppy petals over there on the table.

His face is bare.

His jaw.

His cheeks.

His mouth.

Everything inside Jeanne comes crashing down, just when it was about to pounce.

She looks at him and something in her eyes that welled up in anger surges into a huge spate that spills over without a sound.

22

Private Toussaint Caillet, 6th Infantry Regiment, is wounded at Verdun, Côte de Poivre, Meuse (55), 9 December 1916.

He is struck in the face by shrapnel.

After eight hours spent on the battlefield lying against the sides of a shell hole and then crawling for one kilometre in an easterly direction, he is found during the night and evacuated to the nearest first aid station by Private Buy-Duy and stretcher-bearer Bakker.

The injury is very nasty. Fragments of bone and tooth accumulated in the trachea are likely to have caused partial asphyxia in the first few hours. Because of the cold, the quantity of blood and saliva that has leaked onto his chest also means there is a danger of bronchial pneumonia. Caillet shakes from head to foot for seventy-two hours.

At the first aid station his wounds are disinfected as a matter of urgency. From this point on, treatment will be administered as best it can but the medical teams, being short-staffed, exhausted, underprepared and ill-equipped, are struggling to cope with the substantial influx of casualties. There are a lot of deaths but, as with many who have facial injuries, Caillet's life does not appear to be in danger.

It is nine days before it is possible to consider evacuating him to the surgical ambulance. During this period, feeding remains all but impossible and can be done only in liquid form. Pneumonia is avoided, but asepsis is difficult to maintain.

The surgeon in the ambulance takes stock of the patient's condition. His colleagues at the advanced post have not managed to stop the extensive wound from evolving into a messy pool of foul-smelling pus. Meanwhile the scarring process, which is intractable and already fairly advanced in some places, has formed significant stretches of fibrous tissue. This tissue is starting to thicken and has become inflexible.

A letter is sent to his wife, a flower-maker in the 2nd arrondissement in Paris.

Caillet is pronounced fit to be transported and is evacuated to a surgical centre for internal maxillofacial reconstruction. During the course of his journey to the capital, an under-chin pouch is attached to collect excess saliva. The bandaging around his head, which is kept tight, shrinks as the saliva dries, and pinches painfully.

The patient arrives at Val-de-Grâce, desperately thirsty, two days before Christmas. Despite the cork bung that has been kept between his teeth, his jaws are starting to constrict.

In his notes it says, 'Mutilation of the cheek and corner of the lips; upper jawbone shattered.'

The shrapnel entered through the top lip and exited through the right cheek. On its trajectory the projectile broke the premolars, and shredded the mucous membrane on the roof of the mouth, part of the tongue and a section of the right upper jawbone.

The cheek has an irregular-shaped wound stretching from the corner of the lips to the masseter muscle. Secondary wounds radiate out in all directions.

Caillet is photographed, before being taken to the prosthetics laboratory. He is positioned lying down on the operating table, his head is wrapped in a wet cloth and rubber breathing tubes are inserted into his nostrils. His face, including the wound, is coated in a fatty substance and then the appropriate quantity of plaster is poured over it.

During the drying time, as sometimes happens, the patient starts to panic. His movements make the mould unusable, so the procedure has to be repeated the following day with additional staff in attendance.

Using this mask, a wax model is created demonstrating Caillet's specific injury.

It will be kept at the hospital.

For several months the surgeon observes the different stages of natural scarring and battles to stop the jaws constricting by means of a mouth-opener. The patient is fed on broth and then thicker soup through a feeding tube and then, as soon as possible, with a rubber feeding cup.

The first operation, performed under a cocaine-based local anaesthetic, is for the removal of areas of harmful and inappropriate scar tissue.

The second is to prepare for future reconstruction of the corner of the mouth and mucous surfaces.

Department 5 has recently abandoned grafts using cartilage from sows or calves in favour of grafts from the patient himself. The results are encouraging and the patient, although initially hostile to the method, eventually lets himself be persuaded.

Under general anaesthetic, strips of cartilage are taken from the sixth and seventh ribs, on the same side as the lost facial structures. The advantages of these strips of cartilage are their natural curvature and their malleability.

Numerous subsequent operations focus on rebuilding the shattered jawbone using fragments of rib, and reconstructing the cheek and corner of the mouth with a jigsaw puzzle of successive autoplasties. To fill the significant hollowing in the patient's cheek, an egg-sized quantity of fat taken from his buttock is injected into the area.

Lastly, a foreign body is detected by chance during one of the patient's X-ray sessions. It is a lower molar which was torn out by the initial blast and has buried itself inside the tongue. This almost intact tooth is easy to extract.

An appreciable improvement in the patient's comfort is observed after this extraction, but he then obstinately opposes any further intervention. Against the surgeon's advice and despite what is deemed fairly satisfactory progress, the reconstruction process is therefore stopped before completion.

A prosthesis is inserted to replace the missing teeth. However, mastication and speech continue to prove difficult.

23

They go to the nursery school together to pick up Léo. They left on time, jumping to their feet in a feverish sort of rush. There'll be no waiting in the covered yard for the child today.

It's such a long time since they've walked side by side.

For the first few paces on rue de la Lune, just outside the house, Jeanne's tempted to let Toussaint walk a little ahead of her, because she's still brimful with the ocean swell of images and tears. She's forgotten how to stand by this man's side.

In Toussaint's hair on the flat of the back of his head are the thin white cotton ties that she tied for him just before they left. She slows to watch him walk on ahead, to have something to give her purchase, his shoulders and back, but he stops and waits for her without turning round. So she starts walking and her eye is struck again – as it was on that October evening when he appeared in the doorway – by the disturbing impression that he's grown.

They walk shoulder to shoulder in the dusk. They don't touch but, despite the chaos of paving stones and obstacles in the road, try to step in time with each other. And in her breathless impetus, Jeanne unconsciously adopts the same posture as Toussaint.

Even though there's a noticeable excitement hanging in the Paris air this afternoon, she shuts herself off from other people and their inquisitive peering. She tenses the muscles in her neck. Focusing all of herself on her legs, she places her shoes on the ground cautiously. And walks through the city with these childlike feet, as she once used to cross fields of maize around Replonges.

On the edge of the covered yard Jeanne heads away from the other mothers. As she entered the playground she greeted some with a quick nod, but then hurried on before she could see the surprise on their faces that she, Jeanne Caillet, mother of Léonie, had a man with her. And that sort of man to boot.

The bell has just rung and the schoolyard resonates with the dark choppy waters of swarming children. Somewhere, Léo is buried in the racket and substance of the others. From force of habit, her mother's adept at quickly picking out Léonie in the welter of berets, capes and pinafores. She soon spots her narrow back over there, skipping under her two short plaits.

But Toussaint has no experience of all this, this territory filled with shrieks and babble and movement. He knows his daughter only mumbling quietly on her own with her petals, surrounded by silence. It hasn't occurred to him that she is so different from, and yet so like, other children of her age. Jeanne stands still and holds her daughter with her eyes, while he is disorientated, still anxiously looking for the child.

And despite wanting to avoid the busybodies' curiosity, Jeanne stands very close to him, just in front of him, their clothes rubbing together when one or the other of them stands a little taller to see more clearly. Toussaint is right behind her, heavy and solid. She can hear his breathing, half of it gusting outside the mask. She can feel his quivering, his uneasiness, and discovers that she herself is comparatively solid.

When Léo finally emerges from the melee of the pack and heads towards her, Jeanne guesses from the child's casual lolloping stride that she hasn't yet noticed the unexpected figure waiting in the background. To demonstrate what's left of her resentment, the child just drags her eyes and her shoes along the dusty surface of the playground.

And then she's there.

They're all there, the three of them. Not sure what to do with their eyes, or their mouths, each in their own way.

Léo is suddenly shy, fretfully rubbing her fingers over dirty marks on the front of her chequered pinafore. Jeanne is about to turn round when Toussaint leans forward, brings one hand in front of the child's face with a flourish and opens it. It reveals a cylinder wrapped in rustling paper, broken clean in two but still shining despite the two years it has spent in the pocket of a military coat. It's a stick of sugared apple paste.

They walk to rue de la Lune in silence. They wend their way, all of them awkward. Every now and then the child, who's usually so talkative at the end of the school day, forgets how unusual it is to be going anywhere like this, accompanied by both her parents. And she breaks the silence with a happy, spontaneous click of her tongue that she swallows back down the moment Toussaint's face turns towards her with its sling of white.

They go all the way home and climb up the flights of stairs, the three of them forming just one ageing, exhausted body.

Toussaint hangs up his coat, which is now permeated with the cold, rummages about in the storeroom and riddles the dozing stove. He lets mother and daughter resume their usual pattern. There's a strange density to the air.

Jeanne takes a deep breath. As she pulls off Léo's cape, she kneels and says that she was wrong, she didn't look properly, didn't think straight. About the missing flowers, she means. She got it wrong, that's what happened, she didn't look properly, didn't start right. Because, well, they flew away somewhere else. The flowers did. She knows that now. Léo should have said, about Sidonie and the nine poppies the day before.

Léo unclamps her jaws, yes, she came in, Sidonie did.

And Jeanne nods with a hollow smile.

Before going back to work she picks up the three jugs on the sideboard and sets them down gently, one after the other, on the tiles at her daughter's feet. They overflow with huge flowers, like trophies, illustrating fifteen years of miracles. Jeanne's treasures from the very start.

Her first cornflower in silk muslin, then a peony, a camellia, a Chinese primrose, sweet peas, a hyacinth, six different varieties of rose, lilac, clematis, an arum lily, a carnation, a ranunculus and an intricately veined lily. Lolling over to one side there's even a poppy with a contorted stem and petals in a spectacular orange, as vibrant as poison.

Set apart from the rest, standing alone in the smallest of the three jugs, burns the glowing torch of a huge dahlia. This one's different from the others. It's more than a flower. It's a gaping presence, a bite mark. This dahlia was made in April 1913, on the last day of Bella's sickness. Jeanne can't look at this particular flower without spontaneously hearing the stutter of her first child's poor sighing breath.

The trio of jugs waits on the ground and Jeanne asks Léo to choose. One of these wonders is to be hers.

Till now the child has scarcely been allowed to lay eyes on the top of the sideboard. These flowers have seemed far more sacred than ration cards for charcoal or sugar, and now she must choose her favourite. Jeanne suggests a few options. This one with its beautiful pink flower head, or this one, look at the colour, anyone would think it's still out in the sun.

But Léo purses her lips. She doesn't know. She slowly points at one, then the other, unable to decide. Jeanne stands up, turns the heater back on, washes her hands with soap and prepares to get back to work.

At this point Toussaint takes a step forward, reaches out his hands, lifts Léo up and sits her in the middle of the bed, where he's straightened and smoothed the eiderdown. Seeing him moving like this, in contact with the child, Jeanne senses how surprised he is by the very substance of his daughter, the kittenish weight of her, her natural tendency to flit across the room like this, launching her feet under the corolla of her pinafore.

The child sits solemnly, wide-eyed, her fingers still clutching the stick of apple jelly, and Toussaint suddenly buries her under the flowers.

At first, as he empties the contents of the three jugs one after another onto the bed, there's a manic flurry of colours splurging into each other. But Toussaint assidu-ously finds just the right place for each one along Léo's outstretched legs. Some of the flowers he brings playfully up to his nose with a nod of his head, and he smells them, resting them gently against his moustache and the edge of the white mask.

Sitting at her table with her hands still working, Jeanne cranes her neck to see more clearly.

And Léo relaxes, gives the beginnings of a grimace, a crumpling that might equate to a smile. Toussaint leaps up. He rifles through the darkness of the storeroom until he unearths his old kitbag, then brings it to the bed, where he searches all its pockets. He's found it. A tiny bulging envelope, which he opens carefully. The light from the lamp is not really adequate.

On the other side of the room, the stalk revolves mechanically on its axis between Jeanne's fingers, wrapping itself in a thin covering of cotton.

Various things have appeared on Toussaint's open hand: a cluster of dried petals, a black beetle with broken legs, two seed hulls from trees, but he doesn't know what type, a tiny fossil and an almost intact upper molar.

Extricating herself from the tide of flowers with uncharacteristic care, Léo crawls over to her cot and, quickly returning with her drawstring bag, sits back in exactly the same place. The babbling held in check for more than an hour bursts out of her like a volley of feathers. The room is full of birds.

And now she picks up the flower she's just chosen from among the most luxuriant and, propping it against her pinafore, starts poking her treasures between its petals one after the other: Carnation, Big Green, Mimi Toto, Duck, Big 'sturtium and Little 'sturtium, Mimosa and Radish.

Toussaint bashfully edges his open hand nearer. The seedlings are now joined by these animal, vegetable and mineral fragments, modest trophies of war.

There on Léo's lap, Bella's dahlia looks like a garden.

24

It's as if they've been waiting all day.

They ate their thin soup and the bread. Toussaint sat fidgeting on the armchair reading the newspaper, nodding his head and occasionally letting his eye drift over the patterns in the wallpaper while he pondered nervously.

Jeanne worked without a sound.

Léo grew bolder and, in the middle of the afternoon, she plonked the coffee grinder on one of her father's knees, the one that wasn't jigging. After being bathed in flowers she wanted him to come up with a new game for her. Toussaint opened the grinder's drawer and the two of them peered inside, sniffing it and turning the handle with nothing to grind. There wasn't a single coffee bean left in the room and neither of them found anything to grind other than the air trapped inside the box, which was saturated with a wonderful pre-war smell.

Through the wall, Sidonie's sewing machine purred in fits and starts.

In the end Toussaint left the child holding the coffee grinder and turned to the mirror. He undid a tie at the back of his neck and lifted the mask. Working briskly and precisely, he shaved himself with a little soap and water, without showing his face, as he's taken to doing since coming home.

He pared his fingernails with a small sharpened knife. He tinkered with the Pigeon lamp to repair its wheel, which had been jammed for months. The Pigeon lamp. He's always liked its sugary, very yellow light. Out of the corner of her eye, Jeanne watched him run his first finger over the engraved words: 'Mr Pigeon will give a guaranteed 10,000 F to anyone who makes a Pigeon lamp explode.' It's such a long time since she's had any petrol to put in the thing.

Next, Toussaint patiently set about peeling off the strips of paper that Jeanne had stuck to the windowpanes months earlier to stop them shattering if a bomb landed nearby. Dabbing the glass with a damp cloth and then scraping it with a blade, he seemed to be giving an assurance that the explosions would be stopping forever.

Jeanne meanwhile was at her flowers. It was Sunday, but she had to do something to catch up with the work that had accumulated over a few days.

Catch up with the work, fill the space and the hours.

Poppies appeared in her hands and went to perch on the drying line, perfectly curved and delicately pink. It was almost a miracle. Her fingers and tools were completely focused on her work. The rest of her – Jeanne wasn't so sure.

They were waiting.

And then, at last, Léo slipped off to sleep, tipped back in her cot, sucking on her rag doll's arm. The gaggle of petals and feathers, their ranks swelled by Toussaint's offerings, had returned to the quiet of their bag, while the chosen dahlia, which was too rotund to be stowed in there, shared the child's pillow, as dark and quivering as a huge sea urchin.

Jeanne.
Toussaint.

They're alone and their bodies fill every scrap of space in the room. Toussaint comes and settles himself on the bed, but not under the eiderdown. He leans against the wall, and even though he's already read and reread his *Petit Parisien* he holds it wide, so that it hides him.

Jeanne curls and crimps and sticks and assembles and turns and hangs and lays down her poppies until the middle of the night. She hums to herself and yawns, her bones burning with exhaustion.

From time to time, still sitting up, Toussaint lets himself drop off. The pages of the paper fall onto his corduroy trousers, revealing his head lolling on his chest, his too-long hair that stands up in tufts on his head and hangs more softly below his ears.

Jeanne is thoughtful. The white mask sucks up all the light.

She remembers the man he once was. The man who could tame the darkness around her at the Épatant or the Phénix-Cinéma, where they went every so often before the war. She thought the same thing every time: the heat of him; his mouth, in the dark. You'd never find a more beautiful mouth than Toussaint's.

And now he's like a puppet forgotten in a corner, a punctured balloon.

Without actually thinking the words, she can see perfectly well that this man sitting on her eiderdown has nothing of the hero about him. She realizes that Toussaint most likely didn't kill a single one of the Boche, maybe he didn't even come face to face with any of them, other than with their corpses. Her husband didn't kill or save anyone, he's still covered in mud, fleas, cold, noise, diarrhoea and terror. The war burrowed into him and he's still empty because of it.

He's a huge void, and Jeanne doesn't know whether it can possibly be filled. Whether the two of them are up to it.

She thinks about the great waste of men.

She thinks of her elder sister's husband, the father of four boys, shot down in the first weeks of the war. Of her brother, who was born the year after she was, with deformed legs. Exempted from service, he stayed on the farm with their parents, a scorned, withered figure. She thinks of the lame and the armless. The missing. Those shot to set an example – she's heard stories about some of them. The gassed. Those all around who lost their minds. And the dead, all the dead.

She also wonders if there'll be lots who, like Toussaint, can't describe the violence they experienced, whether or not because of injury.

She thinks of the sad heroes.

*

The sewing machine and the singing from Sidonie's rooms have fallen silent. Jeanne also thinks about Sidonie. Time will have to pass before she gets over it, poor Sidonie.

When her cat eventually died the year before, the seamstress left it on the floor with its stiffened legs and retracted lips until it emptied itself, the fleas abandoned its body and it started to smell like carrion, and Jeanne took it out herself.

She looks at Toussaint, what's left of him. His feet like two black logs upright in the middle of the bed. His shoulders, which rise in waves with his expansive breathing. The curve of his relaxed wrists, the hairs on his arms as supple as waterweeds, his veins. His skin. And she remembers the salty, meaty taste of it.

It's half past two in the morning and, as if settling small children in a cradle, Jeanne finally nestles the last of the poppies amid the crumpled tissue in the box.

She stretches her arms towards the ceiling, stifling a groan, wipes her green-stained mouth, then takes off her bodice and skirt, shakes out her undershirt and unties her plaits. She lays the still-warm fox fur over Léo's legs.

Then she goes over to him, to his side of the bed. Her footsteps are assured, she's played this out in her head so many times while her hands were still back there, busy with their flowers.

His eyes have opened again, he's sat himself up and chucked the newspaper towards the foot of the sideboard with a noisy rustle.

He lights the Pigeon lamp; she goes to blow out the oil lamp, without wondering where on earth Toussaint can have found petrol. The darkness intensifies, then retreats, and soon their every move is bathed in a rime of light.

She unties the mask, one knot and then the other. Her arms form a circle around his fragile head.

And Toussaint lets her touch him, the rasp of his distorted moustache, the part of his lips that is still full, his bluish chin, his neck thick with breath and blood.

He blinks a reply to her unspoken question, he says she can, it doesn't hurt. With the pads of three fingers she starts to read his cheek, venturing as far as the temple and back down along the ridges.

The right-hand corner of his mouth is obscured by a thick, starkly white tongue of overlaid flesh. A long, grainy cleft, its edges still reddish, heads diagonally up to his unharmed ear.

Jeanne explores it with her eyes and her hands. She leans in and Toussaint closes his eyes, she leans closer and he takes her by the shoulders and rolls her over. He weighs down on her with his man's bulk, and she brings her mouth to rest on him in a slow caress.

As she touches it with her tongue, Toussaint's new skin spells out an orange-peel surface, fragrant with its own untamed smell.

25

The light of a new day appears through the net curtains: 11 November. At eleven o'clock the first cannon shot reverberates.

The armistice.

For the Caillets, as for many others, the word is new. To their ears it's only a few weeks old, a few months at the most. It crackles, whistles and cuts like a blade.

The battle is over and the country's jubilation is palpable. They open a window and persuade themselves that even the mist, the roofs and sky are different.

Mills, factories and offices have let out their workers, schools their pupils.

Jeanne tells her daughter the news and then repeats it every hour, as if to convince herself, to listen to the words resonating around the room. France has won the war.

They must go out.

At first, Toussaint plans to go outside without his mask, wearing only his old cap. And then, just as he steps onto the landing, while Jeanne and Mother Birot are putting a shawl over Sidonie's dazed shoulders next door, he turns back. Léo watches him get ready in front of the mirror, restoring his usual colours. The white in its proper place, smooth and clear-cut under the nigella of his eye.

When the child saw her father's bare face for the first time this morning, her slow stirring exploded into a gasp. Her mother was consulted, in silence, to check. And Jeanne nodded.

And then, glancing quickly at the portrait of the soldier on the wall, Léo made a smacking sound with her lips and flopped back down onto her sheet, whispering secrets into the fox's dry ear in her soft voice.

The war is over. They must go and see.

The two women draw the seamstress from her lair, patiently and firmly, swaddling her in wool, honey-gentle arms and kind words. The bells are ringing at Our Lady of Good News and Sidonie swivels round, her face like a panic-stricken bird's.

She's stopped responding, she's empty, empty for all time, poor Sidonie. She has no one left to give. But she goes with them. Mother Birot has her by the elbow.

All five of them finally descend the stairs, preceded by and joined by other tenants.

They go outside. They're on their way, at last.

Now they stream up the avenue des Champs-Élysées with thousands of other people in a great tide of flags. There's shouting and sputtering in the crowd under a foam of hats, confetti and pennants. By a newspaper stand people fight over the *Paris-Midi* and read out loud as they walk along, stunned. People cling to street lamps and lean out of windows. The few cars weaving through are mobbed. Dressmakers wear red, white and blue ribbons around their foreheads. The Spanish flu, which is prowling around Paris, is forgotten.

Off we go. Here we are.

Toussaint goes to buy his daughter a pennant in among all the jostling bodies, and on the strength of his mask he's given it for free.

Hour by hour, the crowd swells. Lots of people are crying and lots of people are laughing. Jeanne does both, she cries and smiles, sometimes at the same time. Next to her a woman keeps on and on saying the same worn, faded words with no trace of anger: Ah, if only they were here, and she lays her hand on Jeanne's arm, expecting nothing in return.

All they can make out of Mother Birot and Sidonie a little way away is their two heads of hair huddled together, white and black.

The Caillets are now just a couple with a little girl, surrounded by other Parisians.

They walk. Perhaps they *are*.

And Jeanne realizes that this morning for the first time the cannon shots that were fired didn't wake the terror that's been churning her insides for months. As if there were several different ways they could thunder, or some unsuspected intuition in the softness of her flesh.

The pain in her foot has eased too, since Toussaint got his expert hands on her wretched National Shoes a little earlier.

He took care of every bit of her.

He slowly removed her undershirt, gazed at her skin and with the flat of his hand stroked the reddened welt under her breast made by the handle of her tool, stroked it again and again. He looked over her body for every single scar from the chickenpox she'd had two years ago.

He pointed to what he hadn't let her see before on his own torso. Gesturing, he explained the neatly sealed wound that showed where parts of his ribs had been taken out, to be fashioned into a fragile jawbone.

They gave each other their wounds.

On she walks.

She doesn't know what she's crying about, what she's laughing about. The armistice won't give her anything back. Reeling and amplified, she laughs and cries at finding herself muddled in with everyone else, as she watches a figure slowly walk away in front of her.

Resisting the flow of the crowd, she grabs hold of a lamp post for a moment to steady herself. Toussaint's tall frame stands out.

She can't see the mask at all, or the ties knotted in his hair. She can see his back, extended by Léo's sharp little back as he carries her on his shoulders, the child fanatically waving her raised arms. In one hand the child brandishes the victory pennant, in the other Bella's dahlia, which she smuggled out under her dress.

Jeanne doesn't know whether Toussaint will be able to speak again some day. She thinks about it, though, here, in the middle of this sea that's dragging all of them along with it. Victory is glorious but levels everything, that's what she thinks. Victory softens personal pain by creating just one national concern. It doesn't listen. And Jeanne wants to listen. She wants to decide, she wants to do things and think.

She doesn't know whether he'll speak again.

Up ahead, Léo turns to look at her, smiling and calling her over.

She doesn't know whether he'll live again.

She clenches her teeth and all the muscles in her face, starts her slow walk again. She's lost her life from before, she knows that. But she'll have to find a way somehow.

Because this is the man she wants.

She closes her eyes. Against her shoulders are other shoulders that carry her forward.

She sees images.

Her white neck against his neck. She slides down, anchors her chin under the bone of his blighted jaw. And, from one voice box to the other, Toussaint hands himself over, it's him, his voice, passing through their layers of skin.

Jeanne will give her own flesh and all the faith she's maintained to help this man come back, *she* will, Jeanne herself, Jeanne and her echo chamber. They'll be two swans with their necks intertwined.

She'll be inventive. She'll help him. They'll know how to cope. Sounds and words might come. They'll start by talking with their skin.

The chapter concerning the ceremony at which certificates were presented to the families of those who died for their country is based on speeches by Ferdinand Brunot and Philippe Maréchal, mayors of two Paris arrondissements at the time. The certificates were illustrated with François Rude's sculpture *La Marseillaise*, which features on one of the pillars of the Arc de Triomphe.

The details of surgical procedures used to treat soldiers with serious facial injuries owe a great deal to the fascinating accounts of surgery performed by Dr Hippolyte Morestin, published in *Bulletins et mémoires de la Société de Chirurgie*, 1915–18.

I would like to thank Sophie Delaporte, as well as Hélène and Christian Platel.

Subscribe

Discover the best of contemporary European literature: subscribe to Peirene Press and receive a world-class novella from us three times a year, direct to your door. The books are sent out six weeks before they are available in bookshops and online.

Your subscription will allow us to plan ahead with confidence and help us to continue to introduce English readers to the joy of new foreign literature for many years to come.

'A class act'
THE GUARDIAN

'Two-hour books to be devoured in a single sitting: literary cinema for those fatigued by film'
TIMES LITERARY SUPPLEMENT

A one year subscription costs £35 (3 books, free p&p for UK)

Please sign up via our online shop at www.peirenepress.com/shop

2021
Peirene STEVNS
TRANSLATION PRIZE

The Peirene Stevns Translation Prize was launched in 2018 to support up-and-coming translators.

Open to all translators without a published novel, this prize looks not only to award great translation but also to offer new ways of entry into the world of professional translation. The winner receives a £3,500 commission to translate a text selected by Peirene Press, the opportunity to spend two months at a retreat in the Pyrenees and a dedicated one-on-one mentorship throughout the translation process.

The Peirene Stevns Prize focuses on a different language each year and is open for submissions from October to January.

With thanks to Martha Stevns, without whom this prize would not be possible.